D1045218

All in the Blue Unclouded Weather

Also by Robin Klein

People Might Hear You
Hating Alison Ashley
Halfway Across the Galaxy and Turn Left
Games . . .
Laurie Loved Me Best
Against the Odds
Came Back to Show You I Could Fly
Tearaways

All in the Blue Unclouded Weather

Robin Klein

Viking

Penguin Books Australia Ltd
487 Maroondah Highway, PO Box 257
Ringwood, Victoria 3134, Australia
Penguin Books Ltd
Harmondsworth, Middlesex, England
Viking Penguin, A Division of Penguin Books USA Inc.
375 Hudson Street, New York, New York 10014, USA
Penguin Books Canada Ltd
10 Alcorn Avenue, Toronto, Ontario, Canada M4V 1E4
Penguin Books (N.Z.) Ltd
182–190 Wairau Road, Auckland 10, New Zealand

First published by Penguin Books Australia, 1991
10 9 8 7 6 5 4 3 2 1

Typeset in 12 pt Sabon by Midland Typesetters, Maryborough
Made and printed in Australia by Australian Print Group, Maryborough, Victoria

National Library of Australia
Cataloguing-in-Publication data:

Klein, Robin, 1936–
All in the blue unclouded weather.

ISBN 0 670 83909 4.

I. Title.

A823.3

Acknowledgements
The verses on pp. 119 and 121 are from the poem, 'Romance' by W. G. Turner, and the words 'All in the blue unclouded weather' are from the poem 'The Lady of Shalott' by Alfred Lord Tennyson.

Contents

For Elliott Maxwell

Mum's Girl

'Look who's over there gawking at us,' said Cathy and because she liked audiences, even if it was only that pudding-head Nancy Tuckett in frilly pink gingham, she started to show off upside-down on the turnstile. The letters above the hospital entrance blurred into a long nonsensical banner – *Wilgawaandriverdistricthospital*. You never knew your luck, Cathy thought, spinning. Visiting Hour had just started, so maybe someone important would come strolling in to see a patient in *Wilgawaandriverdistricthospital* while she was being so athletic. The manager of a circus, for instance, who'd offer her a trapeze job with red spangly tights and a tiara made out of feathers . . .

'Stop making an exhibition of yourself – everyone can see your pants!' Heather said and wrenched the turnstile to a standstill. Cathy tumbled off and skinned a knee. She chased Heather angrily across the clover-studded grass and around the kiosk, and a fine way that was for such big girls to behave, the old ladies in cane chairs on the hospital veranda mumbled disapprovingly to each other.

Vivienne didn't want anyone to think she was related

to them when they were like that in public. They were older than she was – Heather, for instance, was in Second Year at high school and should be setting her a good example. She strolled towards Nancy Tuckett and sat on the other end of the iron bench. Nancy Tuckett was too shy to say anything, even though they were in the same class at school. Vivienne looked at her enviously. As well as the pink ruffled gingham, Nancy Tuckett wore white ankle-strap shoes. Her plaits were doubled into loops fastened with pink ribbons which had little picot edgings. Vivienne's envy swelled in her throat as painfully as quinsy.

New clothes rarely came her way; there were three older sisters in between. Grace and Heather were neat and looked after things, but by the time Cathy had outgrown garments, they were more patches than fabric. Like the awful pinafore skirt she wore now. First it had belonged to Grace, who'd ironed the pleats carefully with a damp cloth after each wear, then it was Heather's, who had tried to liven it up with multi-coloured zig-zag braid. Then it was Cathy's disastrous turn, and now it had finally come down to Vivienne, but the hem had been raised and lowered so many times it looked like a graph of permanent Plimsoll lines.

Oh, it was hateful to be poor!

'The hospital garden's nice, isn't it?' she said in a posh, proud voice, to hide her feelings. 'We're not visiting anyone inside, we were just passing. Hot, isn't it? I've got a new gingham sun-dress but I never wore it today because I'm saving it for when we go to the beach. I've got white ankle-strap shoes, too, just like yours, only I haven't broken them in yet.'

Nancy Tuckett reached into her pocket and drew out a beautifully ironed hanky which had a picture of Snow

White printed in the centre. She blew her nose. She always had a cold, even in the middle of summer.

'I saw Smitty outside the pub yesterday,' Vivienne said. 'I don't reckon teachers ought to go into pubs, do you?'

If Nancy Tuckett had an opinion about that, she didn't offer it. She straightened her brooch. It was shaped like a Swiss mountaineer's cap with a pair of tiny black climbing boots dangling from it on chains. Vivienne could have killed for a fascinating brooch like that. Her jealousy felt as though she'd opened a train window inside a tunnel and breathed a chestful of thick, cindery engine smoke.

'I found a lizard brooch over by the gate once,' she boasted. 'Course I took it straight inside and gave it to one of the nurses, but she said finders keepers, losers weepers. I was going to swap it with Isobel – that's my cousin – for two shillings, but she said she already pinched . . . bought one just like it from Woolies. Isobel goes to the Convent. She learns tap-dancing. She can tap-dance up and down staircases.'

Silence. Even in class Nancy Tuckett hardly ever spoke, and once, Vivienne reflected, she'd even burst into tears when Mr Smith asked her to come out the front and read 'Bellbirds' aloud.

'Viv, we're off home now!' Heather yelled from the gate. 'We're walking round the back way over the aqueduct.'

'That's my big sister and I've got to go,' said Vivienne. Nancy Tuckett, in spite of all her finery, looked rather lonesome sitting there doing absolutely nothing, so she added graciously, 'See you at school Monday.'

To her surprise, when they reached the aqueduct pipes, Cathy whispered, 'Why's that silly Nancy Tuckett trailing after us like Brown's cows? Did you ask her home to play?'

'No, and I didn't even know she was following us,' Vivienne said. 'But she'll turn around now and go away. She won't be game enough to cross over the pipes.'

The pipeline emerged from a high bank on the other side, spanned the swamp underneath and then disappeared again into earth. It was thick and black and was supported every few yards by a concrete pylon. Cathy pranced and capered, stopping in the middle section, the highest from the ground, to stand dangerously on her hands.

'Rotten show-off,' Heather said crossly. 'Just wait till she gets to high school next year and she'll know it!' She went over, exaggerating the peril by spreading her arms wide as though it were Niagara Falls down there.

Vivienne followed, because if she didn't try to keep up with what they could both do, they always ran off and left her. She hated the sick giddiness of crossing the pipes with the swamp underneath. Its surface was covered with reed islands that never stayed in the one place, but shifted mysteriously to other sites from time to time. And things you couldn't see plopped and jumped and squirted rings of slimy green bubbles . . . She shuddered and hopped down thankfully on the far side. Nancy Tuckett was gazing after her across the scummy water, and because Nancy looked so lost and gormless she called, 'There's some stepping-stones there that little kids and old ladies use. You can get over that way if you want.'

'Vivienne, *come on*!' Heather ordered bossily, and Vivienne hurried up the steep hill, past the sinister brick building without windows that everyone at school said was the morgue. Heather claimed scornfully that it was just an electric generator, but Vivienne imagined packaged bodies lying on slabs in total darkness and silence. She fled past, not looking, up to the crest of the hill where the others were stealing flowers from the nurses' garden. Vivienne stopped to watch, rather hoping they'd get caught. They thought they were so marvellous – Heather with a sleeve full of Guide badges and Cathy able to climb trees higher than anyone else. It would serve them right if the hospital Matron sailed out like a yacht in her big flapping starched veil, but they climbed safely back over the fence, hibiscus flowers tucked behind their ears.

They went across the road to the river bank where they had a secret place to which Vivienne was forbidden to come. She watched them go, feeling desolate. It wasn't worth tagging along when she so obviously wasn't wanted. They'd play mean tricks. Last time they'd shown her a place on the ground beguilingly spread with armfuls of fern and told her that if she stood on it and made a wish, the wish would come true. But the ferns covered a hole which they'd filled with squishy cow manure.

Soft footsteps padded up behind her, and she twirled around, but it wasn't Matron or anything nasty that had crept out of the morgue/generator. It was only Nancy Tuckett. Nancy Tuckett glanced nervously at a biscuit-coloured cow grazing behind a rail fence.

'That's our cow and she wouldn't hurt a fly. Cathy can even stand on her back,' Vivienne said. 'Do you want to come to my place to play?'

On the whole, it would be prestigious to be able to boast at school on Monday morning that Nancy had come to her house. Although she wasn't very stimulating company, her father was the bank manager. She had a matching maroon fountain-pen and propelling-pencil set in a little leather case, learned piano, and scarcely ever went to *anyone's* house to play.

Nancy Tuckett just nodded mutely. She looked rather bewildered, as though she didn't quite believe that she'd travelled from the hospital garden to Sawmill Road via a swamp without first asking permission from her mother.

'Come on, then,' Vivienne said, squeezing under the fence and taking a short-cut through the fowl-yard. 'What's the matter? Oh, that chook – just boot her out of the way if she goes for you. Her name's Mrs Rochester, like the mad lady in *Jane Eyre*. Did you see that film? All our chooks have names – this one's Freda, and there's Lizzie and Dot and Dora and Lady Jane Grey. Lots more. We're having chook for dinner tomorrow, probably Dora. Isobel reckons she saw this headless chook jump off a chopping block once and scuttle all round the yard, though you can't believe everything that big fibber says. See this hole in the mulberry tree? That's where I hide all my secret things.'

Nancy Tuckett inspected the hole blankly.

'You know, like when you get sixpence to buy your lunch only you spend it on second-hand comics and transfers instead.'

'I'm not allowed to buy transfers,' Nancy Tuckett said. 'Mum doesn't like the way people use spit to make the little pictures come out.'

'What's wrong with spit?' Vivienne said. 'Ooops! Mind that missing step . . . Isobel took it away to carve up into a totem pole.'

Nancy Tuckett got herself up the back stairs and inside. She blinked around at clothes dumped on floors, cats, sashless windows propped open with empty bottles and flat irons, baskets holding unrelated things like skeins of wool and chokoes and horseshoes, swords and daggers decorating a wall, stacks of ragged magazines everywhere, and Mrs Melling sitting in the middle of it all at a typewriter. There was a knitting needle stuck absently through her hair and the enormous front of her floral apron was studded with safety pins holding notes she wrote to remind herself of urgent jobs. Usually she forgot about them, in spite of the pinned notes. She didn't even look up when Vivienne and Nancy passed through the room.

'My mum writes newspaper poems for when people die,' Vivienne explained, going into the kitchen. 'She's working on one for Mr Humphreys; he got squashed to death under a big frozen carcase at the Meat Works. Cathy said they should carve "He Bravely Went to Meat Death" on his tombstone. Sit down and I'll make us some afternoon tea.' She levered a scrounging cat from a chair and put down a sheet of newspaper. 'To keep your dress clean,' she said politely and Nancy Tuckett sat down, hoping for nice little biscuits and perhaps a glass of raspberry cordial. But Vivienne poked up the fire, slung a pat of dripping into a big iron pan and began to slice some potatoes.

'I make the best chips at our house,' she said. 'Sometimes if I can't drop off to sleep I get up in the middle of the night and fry up some chips. Mum doesn't mind. I can make Gutsy Drinks, too. Oh, you probably won't know what they are, Isobel invented them. I'll make you a Gutsy Drink while the chips are cooking.'

She wiped a glass casually on her skirt. Then she put in a lavish shake of malt powder, a tablespoon each of red jelly crystals, plum jam, hundreds and thousands, Milo and icing sugar, then she added milk from a jug in the ice-chest and stirred it all vigorously with a screwdriver because she couldn't find a spoon. She tipped the chips into enamel bowls and gave one to Nancy Tuckett. Over her own serving she poured a lake of Worcestershire sauce. Nancy Tuckett picked up a chip and nibbled it. It was very black on one side and raw in the middle, but the other side was delicious. So was the Gutsy Drink, and she burped genteely behind her Snow White hanky.

'Now we can play,' Vivienne said when they'd finished eating. 'You can choose, seeing you're the visitor. What do you want to play first? There's this game Danny O'Keefe invented – he lives just up the road – called "Rin-Tin-Tin with a Rusty Sword", only you mightn't like it all that much. Some kids don't. The way you play "Rin-Tin-Tin with a Rusty Sword" is you get the pot-stick from the copper and swirl it around in the dunny-can, then you chase everyone else and try to mark them on the legs, and then they're out. But you need a lot of kids to play that with or it's no fun. Or we could go down the river and pinch some corn. Or over to the sawmill and play "The Perils of Pauline" – the way you do that is you lie down on the conveyor belt and someone else pretends to shove you along towards the big circular blade, and you have to scream. Only not too loud or the caretaker comes out and chases you with a big hunk of timber.'

'I'd better not,' Nancy Tuckett whispered. 'I might get my dress dirty.'

'Well, we could play something inside, then. There's "Operations". You put this old lampshade over your face. Someone has to pour pretend chloroform down through the top, only watch out if it's Cathy – she thinks it's funny to dribble treacle down instead. Or we could get down my Dad's old cavalry sword and play "Condemned Prisoner at the Block" . . . only Mum mightn't let us. Last time Danny

O'Keefe accidentally chopped off some of Cathy's hair. Or there's this other game Isobel made up. You get inside Mum's big wooden chest and shut the lid and be someone buried alive. And I'll be a grave-digger digging up your coffin ten years later and find you with your face twisted up in agony and your hands all hooky while you were trying desperately to claw your way out only of course it was too late and no one heard . . .'

'I'd better not,' Nancy Tuckett said. 'I think I should get back to the hospital now. Mum said to wait there on the bench till she finished visiting Grandma.'

'I don't think Visiting Hour's over yet,' Vivienne said. 'You can always hear the bell from down here, and it hasn't gone yet.'

'I wasn't supposed to move from that bench,' Nancy said unhappily. 'I'd better hurry. We're going on the bus to see my Aunty Nola next. Thanks for the chips . . . Shouldn't we put that frying pan to soak?'

'What for?' Vivienne said, surprised. 'Just bung it down on the floor and the cats will give it a good lick.'

Nancy Tuckett followed her up the hall, stepping around a hen that had wandered in and was pecking at a Sao biscuit on the lino. It was Dora.

'Oh, poor thing,' Nancy Tuckett said softly. 'Is she really going to be tomorrow's dinner?'

'You don't have to feel *sorry* for her,' Vivienne said. 'She's had a very interesting life. Cathy sometimes dresses her up in old baby clothes and takes her for rides in the pram. And anyhow, we'll give her chopped-off head a nice funeral service and make a little wreath out of honeysuckle.'

Mrs Melling looked up from her typewriter and said vaguely to Nancy Tuckett, 'Oh, there you are, Cath. I want you to run over to Mrs O'Keefe and ask if we can have the sewing-machine back. I've just thought of a lovely costume for the Fancy Dress Frolic. If I made a sort of frame out of wire and covered it with cardboard, then you and Vivienne could dress up like those little cuckoo-clock figures that swivel out to tell what the weather's going to be like . . .'

'Mum, this isn't Cathy, it's Nancy Tuckett and she came to our house to play,' Vivienne said patiently.

'I'm Cathy,' said Cathy, who had just come in, dripping from Heather having pushed her into the river after a fight over hibiscus flowers. 'And I don't want to go up to the O'Keefes. It's bad enough Danny's out in our paddock now and he's brought along all his little brothers. Make Heather go and get the sewing-machine back. I've always got to run the messages! I'm always treated exactly like a slave in this house.'

'That's because you look and smell like one,' Heather said just behind her.

'Goodbye – andthankyouverymuchforaskingme,' Nancy Tuckett said, but Vivienne, rather bored now with her company, had already pushed her gently outside onto the veranda and shut the door in her face. Nancy Tuckett stood looking at the door for a little while. It had stained-glass panels, but one of them was broken and the gap covered with a sheet of cardboard. From behind the door came a cry of, 'Mum! Cathy just poked a dried pea up my nose! Oh, I just hope she falls into the sawmill and loses an arm, then let's see Miss Smarty try and stand on her hands! And what's more – she'd never be able to clap when she goes to concerts, either!'

Nancy Tuckett turned away and went back to the hospital. She was just in time, because the bell was ringing to signal the end of Visiting Hour. Soon her mother came out, face virtuous with self-congratulation from visiting poor old Grandma who was away with the pixies.

'Nancy, one of your socks has slipped right down!' Mrs Tuckett said sharply. Nancy bent and straightened it at once. 'And you've creased your dress, too, you naughty girl, as though I haven't spent all morning with a hot iron getting those frills just right! Push your gold bangle up, Nancy, it looks so untidy down around your wrist. What will Aunty Nola think if you turn up looking like that?'

Nancy fixed her bangle and looked down the road at the Mellings' house.

'I hope that bus isn't late,' Mrs Tuckett said. 'They invited us for four-thirty on the dot . . . Nancy, you've got a little spot of grease or something on the yoke of that dress! What a careless child! Stand still while I see if I can get it off with my hanky. And your fingernails aren't as clean as they could be, I'll just give them a going-over while we're waiting for the bus . . . Don't wriggle, Nancy! You've got to have nice clean nails for when you play your new piano piece for Aunty Nola.'

Nancy Tuckett nodded obediently, but kept glancing down the road towards the Mellings' house. The grazing cow had retreated to a corner, because the paddock was full of squeals. There was some game in progress, kids being chased around and around by another kid enthusiastically flourishing a pot-stick . . .

'If you play your piece really nicely, Aunty Nola might even let you get out all her little china ladies from the cabinet and dust them for her. Won't that be a treat? Won't Mum's girl have a good time?' said Mrs Tuckett.

Nancy Tuckett sighed and didn't say anything.

Something to Drop Stitches Over

The first thing Isobel said when Vivienne opened the door was, 'Is your dad home?' It was said with nonchalance, but she stood sideways on the doorstep with her knees flexed for an emergency get-away.

'Sorry. He's gone off prospecting, if you've come with a message for him,' Vivienne said tactfully.

'She means it's safe for you to come in,' Cathy said with no tact at all.

'Course, it doesn't matter to me if he's home or not,' Isobel said airily, not only coming in, but picking up Mrs Melling's corset from a chair and trying it on even though it was large enough to contain half a dozen Isobels altogether. Before she'd even got herself through to the kitchen she'd read a private half-written letter in the typewriter, examined a stack of bills on a spike-stand, rearranged a vase of canna lilies and pulled such a terrible face at the toddler that it had gone to ground, quaking, under the dining-room table.

'That's O'Keefes' little boy, or at least one of them. We're minding him,' Vivienne said. 'Mrs O'Keefe and Mum and Grace have gone to poor Mr Humphreys' funeral. Oh, it's not fair, just because that stuck-up Grace is the oldest and she's left school, she's allowed to go to all the interesting things in Wilgawa! Heather's been left in charge of us and she's acting bossy and picking on us like anything. I'm glad you came to play, it might cheer Cathy up. She's feeling miserable because every night this week she slept with her cheeks pleated up with sticking plaster to make dimples like Shirley Temple only it didn't work. And she doesn't like living in Sawmill Road, either.'

'I hate it!' Cathy wailed. 'Everyone at school looks down their nose when you say Sawmill Road. And this dumpy old house isn't all that much better than Phyllis Gathin's one.'

'I wouldn't worry,' Isobel said. 'If your dad stays out of the loony bin long enough, he might find a big gold nugget and you can buy a mansion like the Powells. Or one of his inventions might get famous.'

'You'd better not talk about his inventions,' Vivienne said. 'Not in front of Cathy. She had to take the last one up to the Matron at the hospital.'

'It was a bandage roller,' Cathy said bitterly. 'I've never felt so embarrassed in my whole life! He made it out of empty cotton reels on a kind of stand and it had a handle thing on the side so you could roll up twenty bandages at the one go.'

'What's wrong with that, then? I would have thought the nurses would be grateful. It would save them a lot of time.'

'You could roll them up, but he'd forgotten to fix it so you could get the bandages off to use them!'

'Well, there's that plantation he's started – what is it

again, tung-oil nuts? It might bring in a fortune one day. Or pigs might fly . . . Anyway, at least you have a nice big veranda going all the way around this house. I just wish I had it for my tap-dancing practice.'

Isobel grabbed a handful of dates without asking and went through the kitchen door into the laundry where Heather, in one of her tidying up moods, was trying to make sense of the clothes. Weeks of mending and ironing and washing were piled up in there, because Mrs Melling didn't believe in wasting time on anything as mundane as housework. You could hardly squeeze into the laundry at all.

'Oh, it's only you,' Heather said, not disposed to welcome visitors, especially flighty ones like Isobel. 'You've got stuff on your eyes again!'

'I know,' Isobel said with satisfaction. 'I pinched some mascara off Mum's dressing-table. Even though her American soldier boyfriend's been sent back to the States, she still wears loads of make-up. She's got hair-colour stuff, too, so I might have a go dyeing mine red.'

'I don't see how you could dye black hair red,' Heather snapped. 'It would come out looking like liver. Anyhow, dyed hair would look ridiculous on a little girl still in primary school – just as ridiculous as make-up.'

'I wouldn't be in primary school if they hadn't made me repeat a year!'

'And just look at that dress you've got on, plunging down nearly to your navel – it's one of your mum's! I've got a good mind to tell on you, Isobel Dion, going round the streets like that.'

'You're only jealous because you don't have any smart clothes to pinch off anyone when they're out. Geeze, look at you in those shorts! Now me, I always look pretty good in shorts on account of having terrific legs, but yours are kind of . . . well, muscly. Not intending to be rude or nothing, but you look like you belong in a shearing shed wearing those baggy old shorts.'

'No one asked your opinion, did they?' snarled Heather, because she thought she looked splendid in the navy-blue shorts Grace had made her for the last Guide camp. 'And you're not supposed to be here, either. If Dad turns up he'll probably kill you.'

'Garn,' said Isobel. 'I'm not scared of that old bug- I mean Uncle Leighton. He doesn't understand how you've got to practise acting if you want to make it to Hollywood.' On her last visit she'd dressed up as a Red Indian princess. She'd rushed dramatically across the paddock and flung herself at Mr Melling screaming, 'Save me, O Great White Father!' He'd been paring one of the horse's hooves and it had shied and kicked him backwards into a blackberry clump.

'I see you've got a new neighbour over the road,' Isobel said, peering out through the laundry door. 'Wonder how long it'll be before she finds out your dad's a raving lunatic and tries to sell her half a share in a tung-oil nut plantation.'

'She's an awful nosey old thing,' Cathy said. 'She spends all her time peering across the road at us. Look, she's hard at it now.'

An elderly woman sat in a rocking chair on the porch of the little cottage diagonally opposite. The cottage sparkled with paint behind a picket fence, and all the flower-beds were edged with sloping bricks. Net curtains, as stiff as whipped cream, hung at each window, and the weather vane on the roof looked as though it had been polished with Brasso. The lady kept glancing inquisitively over the top of her knitting at the Mellings' house.

'She moved in last week,' Heather said. 'Mum went over to say hello and make her feel welcome, but she's not a bit friendly. I don't think she likes kids all that much. She probably thinks we've got too many in our family – as if it's any of her business! And the O'Keefes are in and out of here so much she might think some of them are ours. She sits there on that porch making out she's watching the cars go by, but I reckon it's just to spy on *us*.'

'Well, then,' said Isobel. 'If it's kids she's counting, we could really give her something to drop stitches about! I've got a real bobby-dazzler of an idea, so just listen. First thing is we'll all walk in turn along the veranda, moving real slowly so she gets a good eyeful, then nip round the back out of sight. Then come back here into the laundry by the kitchen door. Cathy, you can have first shot.'

They watched Cathy's leisurely progress through a crack in the laundry door. She didn't look in the direction of the old lady across the road, but stopped half-way along the veranda to unpeg a cloth from the indoor line, then stopped again further along to pick and suck some honeysuckle growing over the veranda rail.

'That's the ticket,' Isobel said. 'That's exactly the kind of thing we want. Now you, Viv. It's a pity you're so little and skinny, because you're kind of easy to overlook, but at least you've got that bright ginger hair. Sort of toss it around so she takes notice.'

Vivienne went, feeling self-conscious. She didn't much like being stared at, specially with a blatant gaze that practically melted the tar on the road in between the two houses. After she got back to the laundry, Heather went, but without much enthusiasm for this silly game of Isobel's, whatever it was. She stomped around the veranda, thinking of all the housework that needed doing, and if she didn't attend to it, probably no one ever would. Thirteen was far too old to be mucking about with a lot of twittering little girls, and it was always a mistake to listen to that scatterbrain, Isobel.

'We should stop fooling around and get this place cleaned up . . .' she said when she got back to the laundry, but Isobel didn't take any notice. She pushed past and erupted onto the veranda like a fireworks display, not needing red hair to be noticeable. She turned cartwheels the whole length of the veranda, and when she came back through the kitchen she wasn't even out of breath.

'Now what do we do?' Cathy asked.

'Now we all get changed into different clothes!' Isobel said and crammed Cathy into a ragged green dress with a scorch mark down the front, only fit for dusters. Cathy walked around the veranda in a subtly altered manner this time, looking pathetic and woebegone. She dragged her left leg a little and hunched her shoulders, and you could almost believe she was coming home after a stint at a last-century cotton mill.

Vivienne knew she couldn't hope to match a performance like that, even though Isobel had tucked her hair up under a beret and dressed her in a plum-coloured satin blouse Mrs Melling had once tried to revitalise with lazy daisy embroidery. She paraded in front of the neighbour, not knowing what to do with her hands, and couldn't think of anything remarkable except to hum 'God Save the King'.

'If I was King George and had to listen to people who can't even keep in tune when they hummed my very own song, I wouldn't want to be saved,' Heather said nastily back in the laundry. She was being bullied into a gingham wrap-around apron.

'That's the apron the cat had her kittens on,' Vivienne said, getting her own back, but Isobel wouldn't let Heather take it off.

'We'll have a double act on the bill this time, but you can leave all the talking to me,' she said confidently. She put on a fluffy voile dress that no one would ever wear in public because Mrs Melling had bought it at a church jumble sale and they all recognised it as having once belonged to Marjorie Powell, the sawmill manager's daughter. Isobel pushed an old wicker pram out onto the veranda and made Heather go with her. She peered under the pram hood and raised her voice. 'Oh, these rotten little twins!' she cried. 'Nothing but grizzle grizzle grizzle all day and night – don't you get sick of looking after them? I certainly do! Pamela – what's that you've got in your pocket!'

'In my pocket?' Heather said in surprise. 'Who's Pam . . .'

'It's not your turn to have the hanky today, Pamela!' Isobel yelled. 'You had it yesterday, you sneaky great thing! Lauretta had it the day before, and tomorrow will be Beth's turn and the day after that young Kenny's, so today it's *my* turn! Only I'll have to look up the hanky roster to make sure.'

'She's overdoing it a bit,' Cathy said critically. Across the road the old lady was taking off her glasses and polishing them on her apron to see better.

On the way back into the laundry through the kitchen, Isobel hauled the resentful O'Keefe toddler out from under the table where he was having a lovely time sailing blotting-paper warships in a bowl of melted jelly. Cathy, wearing a brightly checked skirt and yellow blouse, was instructed to piggy-back him for a circuit of the veranda, then Isobel dressed him in a little frilled pinafore dress and sun-bonnet and sent him off on a howling circuit of his own.

Then she sauntered out, dressed completely in black. She stopped to pick some of the honeysuckle and called back over her shoulder, 'Jennifer, these flowers will do just lovely to put on poor little Wilbur's grave – what a pity he never made it to his fifth birthday.'

'We'd better stop now and get on with the washing. One of you run down to the woodpile and get me some kindling to start the copper fire,' Heather said sternly when she came back, but Isobel and Cathy tied themselves together in a two-legged race and trotted around the veranda in identical school gym tunics, loudly calling each other Susie and Sally.

Cathy went out in a swimming costume and a big straw sun-hat.

Vivienne wobbled around on a pair of rusty roller-skates, wearing a lairy jumper knitted in a stars and stripes pattern.

Heather, nagged into it by Isobel, put on Mrs Melling's reading glasses and a striped blazer and walked around with her nose in a book.

Isobel wanted to run around with nothing on at all, but Heather wouldn't let her, so she wrapped her hair in a towel turban and minced along the veranda in another towel for a sarong, swaying her hips.

'She's got right up out of her chair and she's leaning over the porch rail,' she reported when she came back to the laundry. 'Oh Grandma, what great big eyes you have, all the better to stickybeak with! Now, for a bit of variety. We'll all get dressed up as boys and go round in a group . . .'

But while they were searching for shorts and dungarees in the piles of clothing, someone knocked at the front door.

'Holy cow!' said Isobel. 'If that's your old man, I'm off!'

'It can't be him,' Heather said. 'He doesn't knock, he always charges in the back way yelling and swearing and carrying on. Probably those O'Keefes come to collect little Gregory and borrow something while they're at it. Mum said not to let them have anything till we get the sewing machine back.'

'I'll answer it, then,' Isobel said. 'Leave it all to me. I'll just tell them your dad finally went off his rocker and he's been carted off to the hospital with a tung-oil nut crammed in his gob so he can't bite his tongue into frothy ribbons and it isn't a convenient time for them to be dropping in . . .'

'I think maybe *I'd* better go,' Heather said, remembering suddenly that she was at high school, learning French and Latin and Algebra, that Captain had recently praised her in front of the whole Guide Company for being so sensible, and that Mum had left her in charge of the household while she went to poor Mr Humphreys' funeral. She went pompously to answer the front door, and when she came back she carried a tray piled high with slices of fruit-cake.

'It was her,' she said, red-faced. 'That old lady from over the road. Didn't say much, just came out with, 'Here, give this to your poor mum.' Then she turned round and went straight back to her place again. 'Look, you kids, I don't reckon we should go on playing this silly game . . .'

'I was getting bored with it, anyhow,' Isobel said.

All in the Blue Unclouded Weather

'Soon as we finish this cake, I'm off to watch Mr Humphreys' funeral.'

A Whole Shilling

Phyllis Gathin sat at a desk all by herself under the map of the British Empire. Nobody would sit next to her because she was a pariah. There was something terrible about her stoic acceptance of that role, like the resignation animals show to pain. Cathy Melling felt vaguely sorry for her, but didn't dare show it. She sat in the desk immediately behind, sharing it with Marjorie Powell, to whose every utterance she paid exaggerated heed. If Marjorie decided to let you be her friend, you could consider yourself among the elite.

She said nothing when Marjorie borrowed her things without asking first. She had one treasure, a pen with a glass handle, the shaft filled with coloured water in which a bubble danced up and down like a spirit-level. She kept it in a little crocheted pouch and didn't leave it on her desk in case someone stole it. Out in the playground Marjorie took the pen from its bag without asking and aimed it high into the peppercorn tree like a dart, then she ran off, giggling. Cathy had to climb up and get it down, so was kept in after school for tree-climbing and made to write the multiplication tables out fifteen times. She didn't explain the real situation to the teacher. Marjorie Powell might not have spoken to her ever again, and Marjorie was her key to moving further up the school social ladder.

Phyllis Gathin would certainly never make it even to the lowest rung. Nobody ever asked her to play, chatted to her, or borrowed her things without asking. She had no treasures, anyhow. She was always alone except at lunch recess when she became the hub of a wheel made up of her younger brothers and sisters. They didn't talk to each other. They sat on the grass a long way from everyone else and Phyllis doled out lunches from newspaper wrapping, slabs of bread coated with dripping or cheap fig jam. They ate with their heads lowered, clutching their rough sandwiches in both hands.

All the Gathins were ugly, especially Phyllis. They had shaggy hair, knees crusted with scabs, and strange, awful clothes. Phyllis sometimes came to school in a taffeta evening dress clumsily shortened and disguised as a child's dress. Once she wore the same red blouse for eleven days running – Marjorie Powell carved a tally score on the edge of the desk. Sitting behind Phyllis in class, you could see a dark ring of grime around her neck, and also minute white beads glued to the strands of her dusty hair. That's why no one would sit next to her – their mothers had written letters of complaint to the headmaster. Sometimes he sent all the Gathins home for several days and they would come back with their scalps reeking of kerosene. Then they would shrink into a smaller, more abject huddle in the playground and lower their chins even more.

'Phyllis Gathin has nits,' Marjorie chanted during Arithmetic, because Mrs Owen was safely occupied on the other side of the class-room giving Stewart Thurlow a clip over the ear-hole for flicking ink pellets. 'Phyllis Gathin has nits and one just fell off on a page of her book!' She said it to Cathy, and Cathy turned around and whispered it to Jeanette Everett and the whisper travelled all around the class-room as quickly as a flame running along a fuse wire. Phyllis Gathin put one hand hastily over something that crawled across the page of her book. Her hand was as pale and fragile as someone wasting away from a serious illness, but Cathy just glanced at it and thought how dirty the fingernails were.

'She's catching it for lunch,' said Marjorie, and sniggered.

'Makes a nice change from bread and dripping,' said Jeanette.

Phyllis Gathin bent her head and pretended to be terribly busy working out sums. Cathy peered at her slyly, and noticed a very odd thing. Phyllis Gathin's profile, against the swoop of her dark hair, wasn't really ugly. It had a sort of eerie strength about it. Long black lashes lay like fans on her high cheek-bones, and underneath the dirt her skin was the colour of freshly made milk coffee. Her lips were a soft, sweet bow, holding no bitterness or malice. She looked, Cathy thought in amazement, vaguely like the plaster bust of Nefertiti in 6A's class-room. Almost . . . beautiful.

No, someone like Phyllis Gathin could never be beautiful or even pretty! Marjorie and Jeanette were pretty with their clean flaxen hair, their round faces and sweet-pea coloured dresses crackling with starch. The only pretty thing about Phyllis Gathin was the name of the street where she lived – Greenforest Lane. A name like that made you think of rustling leaves, coolness, and white butterflies flitting about, though the real Greenforest Lane wasn't anything like that at all. The abattoir was at one end and the railway siding yards at the other, with a few ramshackle houses strewn in between like rubbish fallen from a lorry. It was so unsavoury that parents forbade their children to use it as a short cut.

But sometimes Marjorie Powell would visit her grandmother instead of catching the bus home from school, and she'd walk part of the way there with Jeanette. They'd detour along Greenforest Lane. It wasn't done on purpose to defy their mothers, but to examine Phyllis Gathin's house and gloat over their own good fortunes. The Gathins' house was on stilts in the middle of a paddock which was thigh-deep in a lush carpet of some kind of rampant vine. The vine was an evil colour, like green rat-poison. It licked at the stilts of the house and had consumed any fences that had ever existed. Here and there you could see the shafts of an old cart poking up into the air, or the concealed hump of a wrecked car, and in summer the vine bore large, sickly, cornet-shaped flowers which bloomed for one day and then withered.

The house had a front veranda where tattered coats and chaff bags hung from nails banged into the posts. The steps were broken and under them lived a pack of skinny dogs, so thin you could count each rib and knot of their spines. They would raise their heads when anyone passed and voice a token facsimile of sentry duty, but it was evident that they, too, knew their place in the scale of things.

The veranda always seemed to be swarming with Phyllis Gathin's little brothers and sisters, not doing anything in particular, but sitting about aimlessly waiting. They were just a pale blur of faces, like coconuts set up on a stall for target practice. Sometimes you might catch a glimpse of Phyllis's mother, too. She was a Bad Woman. Everyone in town knew there had been half a dozen Mr Gathins, all of them with different surnames and all of them transient. Mrs Gathin was as gauntly tall and imposing as an Indian chief. Her slanted black eyes could halt you dead in your tracks. She would sit, chain-smoking, on the top step of the veranda and her voice, when she addressed any of her children, was as harsh and raspy as gravel. If she did happen to be sitting there, Marjorie and Jeanette would hurry very quickly past and pretend they'd wandered into Greenforest Lane by mistake.

Once, to her great delight, they invited Cathy to accompany them. Mrs Gathin was nowhere in sight, so they dawdled maliciously. Jeanette's shoe came off unexpectedly and she had to sit down and rethread the lace to make it wearable again. Marjorie spotted a cocoon in a tree and suddenly remembered she wanted one for her nature study collection. It was apparently quite difficult to detach from the bark. Cathy, thrilled at being allowed to walk with them on this occasion, inspected each face, waiting for cues.

'I bet Mrs Gathin's down the pub,' Marjorie said.

'My sister Heather saw her going through the rubbish cans out the back of the Greek café once,' Cathy lied.

'Look at their windows!' Jeanette whispered. 'Did you ever see anything like it? They haven't got any curtains, just sheets of old newspapers pasted up!'

Cathy held her nose and made certain that all the small, quiet Gathins on the veranda saw her do it. 'Pooh! The stink!' she cried. 'They clean out fish and chuck the gizzards in the front yard. And worse – my cousin saw Mrs Gathin empty a chamber-pot right there next to the front steps once.'

'Really and truly?' said Marjorie and Jeanette, wide-eyed.

'Cross my heart and hope to die,' Cathy said.

Maybe, she was thinking, maybe Jeanette might ask me into her house and I can smoodge up to her mum and get a part in the Sunday School concert. Or Marjorie might invite me to her birthday party . . .

But after they grew bored with loitering about in front of the Gathins' house and went up Greenforest Lane into Slidemaster Street and down to the intersection of Church Street, Jeanette turned towards the vicarage with her goodbyes reserved for Marjorie only. Marjorie, not looking back, went one block further along to where her grandmother lived, and Cathy had to face the long walk up the river road and was late home because of spying on the Gathins.

'And just what took you so long?' Mum said, glancing up from unravelling an old cardigan of Grace's to knit into one for Heather. 'The others got home ages ago.'

'Jeanette Everett and Marjorie Powell and me were making plans about the Sunday School concert, so I missed the bus home,' Cathy said smartly.

'The Minister's girl? And Marjorie Powell whose dad owns the sawmill?' Mrs Melling said, impressed, and Cathy knew she was off the hook.

'We went inside the vicarage and had a glass of lemonade and some date scones,' she said. 'And I'm probably going to be asked to sing all by myself at that concert, so I'll need a new dress.'

Mum looked harassed and rubbed her forehead as

though she had a headache. 'Money doesn't grow on trees,' she said snappily, but she was wrong about that, because next day Cathy found that it did after a fashion.

The morning started badly. She had to go and look for the cow which had strayed, so she missed the bus and was late for school. Assembly was nearly over. Old Prat was in an even worse mood than usual and yelled at her to go and stand outside 6A's room. While she waited there, her own class filed past to their room next door and everyone stared at her harrowed face.

'You're going to get the cuts!' Marjorie whispered with relish. Cathy instinctively put her hands behind her back.

'Right in front of all of brainy 6A!' said Jeanette meanly and Cathy's eyelids stung with fright. She hated anyone to suspect she was scared of anything, and blinked rapidly, pretending it was just a speck of dust.

Phyllis Gathin brought up the end of the file, shambling past in her dreadful old sandshoes that didn't even fit. She hesitated, then mumbled sideways, 'If youse turn on the waterworks he sometimes won't.'

'Who asked your opinion, Phyllis Pongy Gathin?' Cathy hissed, and Phyllis flushed from the high-tide mark round her neck right up to her hairline. Then 6A marched in, followed by Mr Pratlow, face tinted like a pumpkin with temper and overwork. He glared at her from under knotted eyebrows and Cathy thought she'd drop down dead from terror, but all he said in a scotty bark was, '*You!* Melling girl – don't ever be late again for Assembly! Go on, clear out.'

Cathy scuttled along to 6B and Arithmetic but Marjorie, who was good at it, wouldn't whisper any of the answers this morning. She'd decided not to be matey today at all, and at lunch-break made an intricate cubby-house with Jeanette at the bottom of the school-yard and wouldn't let Cathy join in. Cathy hung about dolefully, watching. They gathered armfuls of dry mown grass and heaped them waist-high for walls, leaving openings where doors should be. Marjorie picked flowers from the bougainvillea that grew over the fence and stuck a bunch in a glass jar.

'Oh, do come in, Mrs Everett, and have some afternoon tea,' she said to Jeanette in a trilling social voice. 'If you don't mind a suggestion about the Sunday School concert, why not have some of the kiddies act out Joseph and his coat of many colours? Wouldn't that be nice? Marjorie Powell would be excellent as Joseph.'

'Can I be another lady coming to visit with Mrs Everett?' Cathy asked.

'No, you can't! Do you take milk with your tea, Mrs Everett?' Marjorie said, offering Jeanette a chipped cast-away ink-pot.

They both ignored Cathy. She tried once more. The lower part of the school-yard was dotted with playhouses and some of them contained enviable possessions. You didn't touch any of the things in anyone else's cubby, but she went to the best one of all, which was at the moment deserted, and stole a spoutless cottage-shaped teapot. She took it to Marjorie and said, 'Look what I found thrown away in the bushes – you can have it if you like.'

But Marjorie just stared coldly and said, 'That happens to belong to Barbara Sylvester and I'm going to tell her you pinched it!'

'Stop pestering us. Why don't you go away and play with Phyllis Gathin?' Jeanette said.

There were some insults almost too outrageous to be

borne. Only – perhaps it wasn't really an insult, because it bordered on truth. It was all a matter of degree. Her family certainly didn't move in the same Wilgawa social circles as the Powells or the Everetts, but although it wasn't a case of being right down there with the Gathins, she did have one thing in common with poor old Phyllis. They both had to wear hand-me-down clothes.

Did everyone else at school think she was pushy and didn't know her place? Last term she'd been popular, captain of the softball team – they'd won the match against the Convent school and everyone had biffed her on the back. Only, recently, it was all different . . . Marjorie and Jeanette, she thought bitterly, were smart at robbing you of all confidence.

She carried her hurt feelings away and mourned under the peppercorn tree. Most of the other 6B girls were playing skippy on the asphalt, using a length of beautiful new rope that belonged to Barbara Sylvester. She could have strolled over there and insinuated herself into the queue, but how awful if someone said, 'What do you think you're doing, Cathy Melling? It's Barb's rope and she didn't even ask you to play!' One shattering rebuff was quite enough, so she stayed under the tree by herself.

There was another person wandering about all alone in the playground – Phyllis Gathin. She approached the skipping girls and stood watching humbly, but when someone glanced at her she veered away. She inched slowly towards a group playing under the water-tank stands, but they stopped their chatter and stared in hostile silence until she went past. Cathy watched her, but without much interest, as one would idly watch a beetle labouring about on the surface of a pond. Then, to her indignation, Phyllis Gathin approached *her*.

She didn't speak, just sat down on the next section of the octagonal bench that edged the peppercorn tree and scuffled her ill-fitting shoes about in the dust. Cathy stared stonily off into the distance and pretended to be interested in the boys on the other side of the playground playing fighter planes.

'I gotta whole shillun,' Phyllis mumbled. She had, too, and was passing it from one black-nailed hand to the other. Then she polished it with spit and ran it to and fro like a little silver cartwheel across the bark of the tree. 'Took bottles back to the shop,' she said. 'Loaded 'em up in the pram and Billy helped me. A whole shillun I got!'

Cathy watched the fighter planes. Stewart Thurlow was getting clobbered by Mr Smith for dive-bombing Alan Bryant off the roof of the woodwork room. The bell would go soon. English, and Mrs Owen might let them have free reading. That wouldn't be so bad, because she could just bury her head in the book and ignore Marjorie and Jeanette right back. Some insults were too outrageous to be borne . . .

'Youse can buy a lotta things with a shillun,' Phyllis murmured shyly. 'Them hair combs in Osborne's with the blue beads. Or lollies. Or a little pink sugar pig . . .'

The bell rang, fracturing the hot air above the playground. Everyone straggled sweatily to line up, making last-minute dashes to the lavatories because teachers got cranky in the stifling afternoons and weren't genial towards raised hands waving desperately about above heads. Cathy rose and headed unenthusiastically towards the sun-baked quadrangle where the heat surged like a forge fire. Phyllis, exuding a sour miasma of unwashed clothes and neglect, tagged after her and had the temerity to reach out and actually touch her on the arm.

'Want to sit next to me in readin?' she asked. 'You can have all the desk to spread yer book out over – I'll just keep mine on me lap. If she has readin out loud all round the class, you can have my turn, too. You like readin out loud. You're real clever at it – nearly as smart as your little sister Vivienne.'

Cathy, affronted, walked on, but the soft, desperately lonely voice coaxed in her ear, 'Aw, go on, sit next to me! Please . . . Tell you what – I don't want this, I can get plenty more. Here, you can have this whole shillun to keep . . .'

'Okay, then, I will!' said Cathy. She grabbed the shilling, knotted it into a corner of her hanky and stuck the hanky into the elasticised leg of her pants.

'You promise to sit next to me in readin?' Phyllis breathed anxiously.

'Sit next to *you* in reading?' Cathy said with deep scorn. 'I can just see myself!'

She managed to get next to Marjorie and Jeanette in line and showed them the bulge of the shilling, not saying where she'd got it. They were overwhelmingly friendly to her all afternoon. Marjorie let her wear her gold heart-shaped ring for half an hour, and Jeanette patted her on the back when Mrs Owen praised her reading. Cathy knew well enough it was because she had a whole shilling to spend after school, but she basked in their favour like a seal on a beach all through the afternoon. She avoided looking at Phyllis Gathin, who made her usual pathetic attempt at reading, stumbling huskily over even the easiest words. Mrs Owen told her twice to stop mumbling and speak up, then in disgust made her get a fifth-class reader from the corridor cupboard and read that instead.

Cathy thought, I'd be spitting mad if anyone took a

shilling off me! I'd go and tell on them to Mr Pratlow. I'd get Heather and Isobel and Stewart Thurlow on my side and we'd all bash them up after school . . .

But Phyllis didn't even turn around to look at her. She just sat there and made worried little jabs at the baby words with her finger, mouthing them timidly and still getting them wrong until the bell rang.

Cathy bought a bag of wonderful mixed lollies. Marjorie and Jeanette helped her with the selection, then they all went down Greenforest Lane.

'That Mrs Gathin's going to have another baby,' Jeanette said. 'You can see when you look at her sideways. She's got a bun in the oven.'

'What's that mean?' said Marjorie blankly.

'I don't know, but it's very rude.'

'My dad saw her lying in a cattle-pen in the show-ground dead drunk once,' Cathy said spitefully. 'And I heard she had this kid and it was simple-minded so they put it away in a Home. Here, have a humbug . . .'

'They should have sent Phyllis instead,' said Marjorie. 'They got the wrong kid.'

'The Gathins all scrounge around the tip and get old furniture,' Jeanette said. 'Can I have that green liquorice allsort?'

They slowed down as they approached the Gathins' house. Mrs Gathin wasn't anywhere in sight, so they stood in the road, openly staring. For once there wasn't a huddle of little kids on the veranda, and the dilapidated house rotted and weathered quietly away all by itself in the hot sun. They stared at a lean, three-legged dog scavenging about in the rubbish by the front steps, at a broken pram full of bottles, at a tin dish on one of the steps buzzing with blowflies.

'My mum says that old dump of a house should be condemned,' Marjorie said.

'What's that mean?' asked Jeanette, impressed.

'Don't know, but it's pretty serious.'

'Have a peppermint cream,' said Cathy, offering the bag. 'Have an aniseed dumb-bell.' Then, encouraged by the silence, she raised her voice and yelled at the sad house, 'Yah – Gathins all got nits in their hair and stink! Phyllis Gathin pongs worst of all! Everyone in town knows she's got a whole lot of fathers she doesn't even know! Phyllis Stinky Gathin's so ugly no one would ever sit next to her – not even if they got paid!'

But the veranda wasn't empty after all. Phyllis Gathin's face suddenly appeared over the broken railing. She'd been sitting down out of view, but now bobbed up and gazed at them for a moment with her still, dark eyes. Then she put her head down and ran in through the front door, letting it slam behind her.

The three girls turned a little pink and walked on self-consciously towards Slidemaster Street.

'Oh, well . . .' Jeanette said.

'It doesn't matter, anyway,' said Marjorie.

'Course not,' said Cathy uncertainly. 'She hasn't got any feelings like proper people.'

She was thinking about how Phyllis had curiously blank eyes and always seemed to be in perpetual retreat behind them, to some distant place. But perhaps there wasn't a place far enough. Just before Phyllis had fled inside, she'd seen in the depths of those dark wells a little flicker of something that looked like . . . sorrow. It had reminded her of something. There were terrible photographs of concentration camp inmates she'd seen in a magazine just after the war ended. Their faces had all been stamped with a dreadful, bewildered grief, a despair so beyond comprehension that it had made her quickly turn the page to the comic strips instead . . .

Only that couldn't be right. Everyone knew that Phyllis Gathin had no feelings like normal people.

'Got to hurry,' Jeanette said. 'I should have been home ages ago. I'm helping Mummy make some disciple costumes for the Sunday School concert.'

'Matthew, Mark, Luke and John,' Cathy chanted, airing her knowledge. 'Gabriel and Peter.'

'Gabriel wasn't an apostle,' said Jeanette smugly. 'You should turn up more at Sunday School. Mum was noticing how you never show up. You didn't come for four whole weeks. I'm going to be Mary in the concert.'

'I'm going to be an angel,' said Marjorie. 'Maybe I'll get another part as well. The boys all said they won't be in the concert because it's sissy, so everyone else has to play boys' parts.'

'Won't I . . . won't I get a part at all?' asked Cathy.

'Well, you can't not turn up at Sunday School then expect a part in the concert and a present from the Christmas tree.'

'There's still some marshmallows left in the bag,' Cathy said, holding it out.

'You could be one of the disciples, I expect,' Jeanette said. 'They don't really do much, just walk across the stage all together in a bunch. Those Sylvester girls grabbed all the best apostles to be, though. Come in and help with the costumes, Marjie? You can make some of the beards.'

They went in through the white picket gate of the

vicarage and closed it firmly behind them, with Cathy on the other side.

'I'm coming to Sunday School this week,' Cathy called after them wistfully. 'I only didn't go those other times because . . . because we had to go up river and help my dad clear the block. Jeanette, tell your mum I can be one of the disciples. I don't mind a bit acting a boy's part . . .'

'Oh well, I suppose you can be Judas,' Jeanette said over her shoulder. 'No one else wants to be him, he was so awful.'

Judas – at first Cathy couldn't remember anything about that one at all, but as she trudged up the river road towards home, she suddenly did remember. Judas and pieces of silver and treachery. She looked at the last marshmallow in her bag and decided that marshmallows didn't taste very nice, they tended to stick in your throat.

Pay-Back

It was cool and delightful under the house. Isobel kept all her magazines in a box there, and had decorated the chimney base with film-star pictures and a mirror hanging on a nail. She examined herself critically in the mirror, wondering if her mum would notice if she plucked out her eyebrows and painted fake ones higher up. Joan Crawford had terrific high eyebrows, but then she also had a team of Hollywood make-up experts to get them just right. Isobel decided to leave hers till later and get her revenge book up to date instead. When she'd first started it, she'd tried to write the entries in blood, jabbing the ball of her thumb with a hat pin. But she'd never been able to make enough come out, so now she just used red ink. She glanced nostalgically back through previous entries.

'Victim: Heather Melling. Reason: Said I don't look like Dorothy Lamour at all – more like Boris Karloff on one of his bad days and my legs are bandy like a goanna. Pay-back: Wrote 'Heather M. Loves Danny O'Keefe' on hospital kiosk wall.

Victim: Mum. Reason: Walloped me with fly-swat

and I never did anything! Pay-back: Waited till she got comfortably settled on the lav, didn't tell her the dunny-cart man was just coming in at the gate, told dunny-cart man to go right in cos no one was using it.

Victim: Sister Eugenie. Reason: Three-hundred lines just for talking in Mass – how does she know I wasn't praying out loud? Revenge: Not decided yet. Spread a rumour round school that the dunny-cart man's her brother?'

It was hard to concentrate on the entries. The only thing wrong with using this part of under the house as a secret hide-out was not being able to get away from the wireless going full blast in the kitchen directly above her head. It was turned on to the request program, because her mum liked all the sentimental songs people wrote in for. Isobel made cat-sick noises as the announcer said, 'Now, a special request for Mrs Tuckett of Pramble Street – the lovely, evergreen "I'll See You Again".' After 'I'll See You Again' there was 'Hey Mister Sandman, Send Me a Dream' for a Gwendolyn Atkinson who lived up the river.

Isobel filed and painted her fingernails with letter-box red varnish stolen from her mother's dressing-table drawer, and while they were drying flipped to a recent entry in her book.

'Victim: Stewart Thurlow. Reason: Chucked my Esther Williams orchid bathing cap over the fence to a dog. Pay-back: Wrote anonymous letter requesting soppy 'Christopher Robin is Saying his Prayers' for Stewart Thurlow, Roadside Mail Box 48, Upper River Road.'

That had been one of her more successful revenges. Just about everyone heard those requests read out on the wireless and Warty Thurlow was given a bad time down at the baths next day.

Isobel looked at her hair in the mirror and wished it was either coppery blonde like Heather's or auburn like Vivienne's. Auburn hair was completely wasted on that dope Viv, anyhow. Every time she turned up to play, she got her nose stuck in a book instead. Isobel couldn't understand people who read books; there was always far too much going on in real life to waste time on nonsense like that.

She removed a loose brick from the chimney base and took out a tin that held a packet of cigarette papers, a box of matches and some butts collected from the lounge-room ashtray. The cigarette she rolled was really professional, almost as good as a ready-made one, and she watched herself blowing smoke rings in the mirror and pretended she was Joan Crawford. Except she thought she looked much more like Dorothy Lamour. Once she'd sent a letter and photo to a Hollywood studio asking for a job as a stand-in for scenes where they didn't want Dorothy to get her hair messed up or her sarong wrinkled. But all she'd got back was a signed photo of that little smarty-pants Shirley Temple, and she was sure the signature was a forgery – it looked just the same as the ones on her photos of Errol Flynn and Veronica Lake. If she grew her hair long in the front she could maybe wear it flopping over one eye like Veronica Lake . . .

'Isobel!'

Isobel hastily stubbed the cigarette out. She hadn't really smoked much of it, anyway; the taste was horrible, like camel dung, and it always made her cough. She kept still and quiet. Her mum would never think to look under the house, didn't even suspect she had a secret hide-out . . .

'Isobel! I know you're under the house mooning over those film-star pictures! If I have to call you again, madam . . . You come here right this minute and do the messages.'

The shopping list, Isobel thought, was as long as a Lenten sermon. Two boxes of matches, one pound of brown sugar, a knob of blue for rinsing the clothes, starch, flour, bacon rashers, sago . . . 'How am I supposed to cart all that lot home?' she demanded sulkily, fiddling with her hair. She'd read in the *Stars' Beauty Hints* that you could bleach hair with lemon juice, only when she'd tried it had just made her scalp itchy. Maybe you were meant to add a little bit of water to the juice, not just squeeze ten lemons directly all over your head . . . 'Why don't you ever pick up the groceries for a change instead of listening to that corny muck on the wireless?'

'Don't be so cheeky. Why can't you be like that nice little Vivienne, you never hear her answering her mother back. And leave your hair alone!'

'Can I get one of those home-perm kits while I'm down the shops doing myself an injury lugging all those things back?' Isobel asked hopefully. 'Go on, Mum! The ad said you can't tell the difference between them and a real perm.'

'No you can't! Eleven's too young to have a perm. You'll be asking me if you can paint your fingernails next.'

Isobel quickly put her hands out of sight.

'Let's see now . . . a tin of peaches, a large one of plum jam, salt . . . Oh yes, I nearly forgot – we need a new broom. That old one's barely got any straws left in it.'

'I am *not* carrying a broom all the way home through the streets!' Isobel said, outraged.

'You just do as you're told for once without arguing. How do you think everyone else gets new brooms home when they need them? And stop scratching at your scalp! Here . . . you haven't caught things in your hair, have you?'

'Me? Course not!' Isobel said indignantly, not mentioning the lemon juice. Mum had threatened to belt her if she had any more goes at dyeing her hair blonde or red.

'Well, just to be on the safe side you can pop into the chemist and buy a fine-tooth comb. I'll give your hair a thorough going-over tonight.'

'I'm *not* going into the chemist and asking for anything so embarrassing!' Isobel yelled. 'He'll know it's for me and so will everyone else in the shop! What if Sister Eugenie happens to be in there buying something? She wouldn't let me be Our Lady in the Christmas play! Who ever heard of Our Lady with *things* in her hair!'

'For goodness sake, child, go in when the shop's empty and ask for it. Now just get off and do those messages, or I won't give you any money for the pictures on Saturday. I mean it, Isobel! I don't know, I do the right thing and send you to the Convent so you can learn nice manners, and all I get is sassiness and arguing . . .'

'A broom and a fine-tooth comb,' Isobel said bitterly as she snatched the purse, the list and a string bag. 'I bet Dorothy Lamour never had to shop for stuff like that! One of these days I'm just going to run away, then you'll be sorry!'

'Well, I don't know where you'd run to,' Mrs Dion said. 'You can't very well go and land yourself on the Mellings. Uncle Leighton said he'll skin you alive if he ever catches you up there again. Talking Cathy and Viv into going to Mr Humphreys' funeral last week . . .'

'We never! It was all over by the time we . . .'

'The three of you all dressed up in black standing round that new grave wailing and weeping and dabbing at your eyes pretending to be mourners!'

'But all the real ones had gone home. I don't see it matters. No one even saw . . .'

'Grace saw you from the bus. She said she was never so embarrassed in her whole life, Cathy in a black evening dress and a black lace veil. That was your doing, madam, if I'm not very much mistaken! Not to mention . . .'

Isobel left hurriedly. Usually when she was sent on a message she nicked round the back of Tuckett's and borrowed Nancy's bike which was kept in the shed. She never bothered asking, because Mrs Tuckett was so mingy she wouldn't even give anyone a fright if she was a ghost, but that bike was wasted on Nancy. Every afternoon you'd see her out the front of her house trying to learn how to ride it. She'd place one foot on a pedal and wobble to the right, then topple to the ground. Then she'd put the other foot on the other pedal and wobble to the left and fall. She'd been at it for months now.

Anyhow, a bike wasn't much use when you had to carry home a new broom. To put off the utter disgrace of that, Isobel went into Osborne's store when she reached the shopping centre to look at the new hats. They had a lovely fresh tang of new straw and their brims were lined with ruched net decorated with little velvet forget-me-nots. People like Nancy Tuckett wore hats like that to Sunday School, but Isobel considered them babyish. She preferred to create her own from bits and pieces, so she tried on a few from the ladies' hats display to get inspiration. One of these days she was going to make herself an emerald-green turban or a natty little red pillbox with a spotty veil. She left the hat stands and wandered through the corset department, yearning to be old enough to wear a corset. You could pull the strings tight and look as elegant as Scarlett O'Hara in *Gone With the Wind* – except there wasn't anyone like Clark Gable in Wilgawa, so it probably wasn't worth the discomfort.

She inspected some lace-edged hankies displayed on the counter and considered pinching one, but the saleslady was watching her like a chicken hawk. Isobel put the hanky back and pretended she'd only been looking up at the little cash-boxes on their overhead wires. The saleslady would put the docket and customer's money into a wooden sphere, then send the little sphere zipping along a wire to the office, and the cashier would put in the change and whizz it back to the counter. At one stage Isobel could think of nothing more glamorous than standing behind the corset counter in a smart black dress, calling people Modom and being allowed to work those zippy little boxes. But that was before she found out she looked like Dorothy Lamour.

She left Osborne's and meandered around to the Roxy Theatre to check out the coming attractions. A coloured poster announcing next week's film said dramatically, 'They were sisters . . . a scoundrel blighted their lives!' but she thought she might go to the Odeon instead and see *Blood and Sand* starring Rita Hayworth and that gorgeous Tyrone Power. It certainly might be a good idea to stay away from the Roxy for a little while – or at least until she could talk Mum into letting her have a home-perm as a disguise. They had this thing at the Roxy where you could put your name down on a birthday list, and at Interval you got called up on the stage and given a free ice-cream and a slice of birthday cake. Only she'd used a whole lot of made-up names and birthdays a bit close together, and even though she'd worn something different every week, one of the usherettes had reported her to the manager.

She caught sight of the time on the post office clock and groaned. In the grocery shop she read out the shopping list as slowly as possible, leaving the broom till last. There was a moment of soaring bliss when Jack O'Keefe said they'd run out of brooms, but then he checked in the storeroom out the back and found the last one. Isobel glared at it with loathing. Its handle glittered with new varnish and the thick yellow straw was bound with a double row of red and green twine. It was as noticeable as a Christmas tree, taller than she was, and there was no possible way in the world you could wrap a broom in brown paper and disguise it.

She slunk out into Main Street, carrying the heavy string bag in one hand and trailing the broom from the other. It seemed to her that every passer-by was turning to stare at her. A man having a shave gawked out of the barber shop window, and so did all the people waiting for the East Wilgawa bus outside the post office. Isobel tried tucking the broom under one arm like a baton, but someone walked into the back of it, had their chin stabbed with crisp new bristles and loudly told her off. She carried it in front, but it kept swivelling out sideways and tripping people up. And she still had to negotiate the corner of Station Street where all the main shops were. She thought she'd die of embarrassment having to walk through the crowd of Saturday morning shoppers there, but before she even reached the corner, the broom handle got caught in the spokes of a baby's pram.

'Watch what you're doing – that could have poked him right in the eye!' the baby's mother said indignantly. One of the pram spokes was buckled. Isobel obligingly tried to dong it back into place with the tin of plum jam from her shopping bag, but the baby placed an inquisitive finger in the way. Its howls and the lady's scolding voice followed her around the corner into Station Street.

She flinched. There seemed to be even more people about than usual, because Bailey's had their new summer shoe stock in and people were looking at the window displays. She tried to creep around behind them, unseen, but just then Marjorie Powell came out of Bailey's, full of self-importance and wearing beautiful new patent-leather shoes with bow decorations. She carried the cardboard box where she'd put her old ones. Isobel suddenly realised she'd forgotten to change her own awful old sandals before she'd come down town, the ones that had turned funny and shrivelled looking when she'd tried to change the colour by soaking them overnight in Condy's Crystals. She attempted to bluff her way past, angling the broom-handle nonchalantly over her shoulders, as though she were a milkmaid and two pails hung in a picture-book fashion from either end.

'Sweep sweep sweep!' Marjorie purred. 'Oooh, you do look funny – you and those purple sandals! Has someone given you a job sweeping down the footpaths?'

'Shut your face,' Isobel said.

'Maybe you could sit on that broom and *fly* it home!' Marjorie said very loudly, so that everyone at the shop window heard. A couple of people tittered. Isobel furiously manoeuvred herself, the awkward bag of groceries and the broom around the corner out of sight. If she'd had her revenge book handy, she would have written Marjorie's name down there and then, and in blood, too, even if she'd had to punch herself in the nose to get enough.

'I'm going to pay that rotten Marjorie Powell back if it's the last thing I do!' she vowed bitterly. Only . . . it was probably going to be difficult to pay Marjorie back. She was so cushioned, like one of those big boxed dolls the stores displayed at Christmas, encased in layers of glittering shredded paper so that no harm could possibly come to them.

It wasn't *fair!* Isobel thought, changing the string bag to her other hand because the handle was biting into her palm. It just wasn't fair about that Marjorie Powell! She went to dancing classes, too, and always had the nicest dress at any concert. The last one had been powder-blue net with spangles sewn all over the bodice, and Isobel had been so dizzy with jealousy she'd mucked up the one little solo she'd been given. And Marjorie was forever bringing new things to dancing class and bragging about them, a jingly charm bracelet, a heart-shaped gold ring. Even at the end-of-term break-up party she'd brought in a special mug to drink out of! Her christening mug, the same pudgy shape as herself, silver-plated with her name etched on one side. But the hardest thing of all to bear was that Marjorie's hair curled naturally, bouncing all over her head in little spirals like the wire binding of those shorthand notebooks secretaries used.

Hair . . . she still had to buy that degrading, humiliating, fine-tooth comb! Mum might waste hours listening to all the serials on the wireless and that gushy request program, but she was a real stickler about hair being kept clean. A fine-tooth comb – how could anyone be expected to walk into the chemist and ask for something like that! Isobel crossed the street, too wretched to even care about being seen carrying a broom now, and peeped in through the chemist's door. There was a customer inside, and she certainly wasn't going to ask in front of an audience! They'd look at her, suspecting she had things in her hair like all those Gathin kids in Greenforest Lane.

She hung about in front of the shop, trying to summon enough courage between customers, but every time she nerved herself to go in, someone else would push past and go up to the counter. She pretended to be inspecting the window display of fancy soaps and face washers arranged like fans, but thought that Mr Ingelow inside was peering out at her, suspicious that she'd been hovering there for so long. Oh, it wasn't *fair!* She bet that Marjorie Powell never had to go into a shop and ask for something as shameful as a fine-tooth comb! All those curls adorned with ribbons and flowers on concert nights – once she'd even had a beaut little top-hat sprinkled all over with silver glitter. And her mother always seemed to be bustling about in the dressing room, darting at Marjorie to adjust a curl so that it fell forward over her fat pink cheek, shoving other kids aside so Marjorie could have the full benefit of the only mirror . . .

Mr Ingelow really was glaring at her sternly. In a minute he'd come out and demand that if she intended to buy something, she should either come in and stop breathing all over his clean shop window, or take herself off. But then several people entered the shop in a bunch, all of them wanting hard-to-get-at items which had to be fetched from top shelves and glass-fronted cabinets. And now he was mixing up a special cough medicine for someone – oh, she couldn't . . . just couldn't ask for a fine-tooth comb in front of all those customers! People would talk about her all over town. Everyone gossiped about everyone else in Wilgawa, starting one small rumour winging on its way to finish up at the other end of town like a plague of grasshoppers. She'd done it herself occasionally to keep her pay-back system up-to-date.

Her pay-back system . . .

A smirk settled on her face, and she suddenly bounced into the shop, making so much clatter and noise that everyone turned to stare. 'Hey, Mr Ingelow!' she yelled.

'In a moment,' he said tersely.

'But Mr Ingelow, I'm in an awful hurry. It's *important!*'

'You take your turn, same as everyone else, young lady. And be careful with that broom, you'll have those packets of Aspro all over the floor.'

Everyone eyed her with disapproval, a loud-voiced, pert little girl trying to push her way out of a queue. Isobel didn't mind one bit. She flashed them her toothy Dorothy Lamour smile.

'It's very *important*,' she said, lifting her voice so that everyone could hear, all the people in the shop and out on Station Street and maybe even the whole of Wilgawa. 'I need a fine-tooth comb *urgently*. You know – one of those combs people use to get nits out of their hair. Mrs Powell asked me to buy one – it's for her daughter Marjorie.'

The Visitor

'She's our cousin, too, even though we've never met her!'

'Rita's the same age as me and we won't want a lot of stupid little girls butting in on our conversations,' Heather said and continued smugly with what she was doing – dumping their bedding on the veranda. 'That's why I've decided you can sleep out here on the camp stretchers while she's staying.'

'Anyone can climb in over the veranda rail,' Cathy said indignantly. 'We could wake up and find we've been murdered in our sleep!'

'Good,' said Heather. 'Neither of you would be much loss to the world. I hope I've made things clear – I don't want you hanging about bothering Rita and me. We'll have a lot to talk about.'

'You've never even met her, either!'

'*I'm* the one she's been pen-pals with for two whole years now, and we're practically bosom friends through our letters. You two certainly won't have anything in common with her! For a start, Rita's very refined. She learns elocution and violin and paints the most adorable little water-colour pictures for people's albums. While she's here she's going to do me a lovely crinoline lady in a garden holding a parasol. I want everything to be perfect, even if she is here only for a night and a day, so as soon as you finish putting up those stretchers, you can take the hall mat outside and give it a good shake.'

'Why can't *you*?'

'I'm going to make some delicious patty cakes for me and Rita to have for supper after you're both in bed.'

Cathy and Vivienne stuck their tongues out at the closing door. Cathy went one better and put her thumb to her nose and waggled her fingers about. 'Big bossy-boots!' she muttered. 'You should see all the whopping great fibs she puts in her letters to Rita, too. I hold them up to the lamp and read through the envelopes. She reckoned she got a special Girl Guide bravery medal for saving someone in a bushfire, and Dad owns a cattle-station. Putting on all those airs – you'd think Princess Margaret Rose was coming to visit!'

'Not only that,' Vivienne said. 'She's going to draw charcoal seams up the backs of her legs so Rita will think she's got a pair of nylon stockings on. Acting so grown up and making us stay out of the way, not even letting us go down and meet the train tonight. Let's just ignore them both when they get back!'

But when Mum and Heather came home from the station with Rita and her suitcase, they were hovering about in the hall, openly staring. They'd thought that someone who learned elocution and violin and lived in the city would be somehow exotic. Vivienne had a hazy mental picture of Rita carrying a little fur muff even though it was mid-summer, but the real Rita was frankly disappointing. She had large front teeth and pale eyes that blinked a lot behind sandy lashes. Her dress with its Peter Pan collar was no different from anything you could buy in the Wilgawa stores.

'Stodgy and podgy like tapioca pudding,' Cathy and Vivienne whispered to each other and stopped feeling resentful that Heather had appropriated her as a special guest. As far as they were concerned, Heather was welcome. Rita's conversation was as colourless as cellophane, and after tea she didn't want to play games outside, but opened a little sewing-basket she'd packed in her suitcase. She took out a supper-cloth she was making for her mother's birthday, and they suspected she'd brought it along just to show off. The work was so neat and meticulous you could have sworn it had been painted on with a fine camel-hair brush. Vivienne, who'd spent a whole term at school being made to unpick and resew one simple French seam, knew then that she and Rita couldn't ever possibly have anything in common. She retreated to the table and played a game of Consequences with Cathy, even though it wasn't much fun with just two.

On the other side of the room Heather chatted brightly about various things, Guides and swimming and school, but there was a forced quality in her voice, and Vivienne felt a bit sorry for her. Rita somehow capped every remark she made with a better anecdote. She was in Guides, too, but it came out that she had twice as many badges as Heather and they'd sent her embroidery to be part of a special interstate exhibition of Guides' handiwork.

She was also a big nosey parker, Vivienne decided, noticing how her eyes kept rambling around their lounge-room. Even though Mum had made a huge effort and tidied the house specially, Rita's probing eyes fastened on little things like the shabby blind that had lost all its spring and was clipped up out of the way with a clothespeg. And the eccentric bead curtain in the hallway arch which Mum had made from painted cotton-reels and ping-pong balls and gumnuts threaded on twine. She was staring now at the chalky plaster surround of the fireplace, craning her head sideways.

'Yes, Aunty Connie, the Gibsons still live in Frederick Street,' she murmured politely to Mum. 'They said to give you their regards. Old Mrs Gibson still remembers you from when you were a girl . . .' But she was examining the fireplace wall while she pretended to thread a needle with pink embroidery cotton. Vivienne suddenly remembered what was there, and felt guilty and mortified. She and Cathy had spent one wet afternoon composing a vulgar alphabet, scratching out the letters in the plaster. A for Abscess, B for Buttock, C for Catsick, D for Diarrhoea . . .

Rita was nearly toppling off her chair trying to decipher the spidery writing.

E for Earwax, F for Flatulence, G for Gizzards, H for Halitosis . . .

'Would you like to play Chinese Checkers?' Vivienne asked to divert her, but a distraction of larger proportion came from the back veranda.

'I thought Dad was going to be away for a couple of days!' Heather said, looking stricken as bags and bales were thrown on the veranda accompanied by loud innovative curses. But when Dad racketed inside demanding tea, making a startling amount of noise for a wiry little man who looked like a leprechaun, he cheered up at the sight of a visitor in the lounge-room. He liked meeting new people.

'And who have we got here? What's your name, Miss?' he bellowed at Rita jovially. 'Speak up, damn it! Ruthie? Rita . . . Oh, you must be that bloody silly Elsie's girl, then! No more brains than a chook, that bloody Elsie!' He sat down and proceeded to earbash Rita for one hour and seventeen minutes. Vivienne and Cathy timed him by the mantel clock, and all Rita managed to get in was one 'Really?' and one 'Ooh, isn't it getting late?'. Dad was telling her all about how he'd fought in the desert and found a Turk's fez with a head still in it like a paddymelon stuck in a bucket. Rita put the needlework away in her little basket and huddled low in her chair, looking restive.

'Dad,' Heather ventured bravely. 'Rita's had a long train trip – I think she'd like to get ready for bed now.'

'Rubbish!' he scoffed. 'Hefty strong girl like her – she could bung up the framework for a barn single-handed and not feel tired, not like you niminy-piminy twerps. Who asked your opinion, anyhow, Miss Gabby? I haven't told her about the time I donged that big snake out in the shed and it shot away under the floorboards, but I grabbed it by the tail and gave one hell of a yank and brought the whole bloody shed down around my ears! Want to know why, young lady? That blighter had its fangs sunk like a vice into a bit of timber and couldn't get them out. You never saw anything like it, unless it was the time I went pig-sticking up near Baroongal Flats . . .'

'Rita, would you like to go to the bathroom before we get ready for bed?' Heather interrupted with determination and Rita nodded gratefully. Heather explained that a vital part of the bathroom was rather a long way down the back near the fowl-house, and she'd need a candle. Rita made the best of it and said that ooh, she'd forgotten she was in the countryside now, and wasn't she silly!

'Nice little girl, that,' Dad said in her absence. 'Knows how to listen and not nag and earbash like you mob . . . Now what's that din – sounds like someone having a fit down the back . . .'

'Oh, we forgot to warn her about Digger!' Heather cried, and ran down through the dark, lantana-scented backyard. She shooed the big horse away from the lavatory and coaxed Rita out. 'It's all right, that wasn't an earthquake, it was just one of the horses. He's got a habit of rubbing against the wall when he gets an itch . . . Sorry, you must have got an awful fright having the whole thing rock.'

'At home we've got a proper inside lavatory,' Rita said stiffly. 'It's all tiled in cream and green to match the bathroom.'

'I don't like that Rita much,' Cathy whispered to Vivienne. 'She's a big drip and I'm *glad* Heather wants her all to herself tomorrow!'

But next morning Heather crept out early to the veranda and woke them up. 'Look, you kids . . . I didn't really mean you weren't to hang around with Rita and me,' she said. 'After all, she is your second cousin as well as mine, and I shouldn't be so selfish. In fact, wouldn't you like to take her down to the park today? I've just remembered I've got a whole lot of French homework to do.'

'Oh? A teeny bit bored with a certain person, are we?' Cathy gloated.

'I never said that! You're only jealous, you little cat, because you don't have any interesting city pen-friends who come and stay with *you*! Rita could have spent the extra time up in Grafton, but she cut her holiday short to stop off and visit *me* on the way home. I'm really sorry she's got to go back tonight and can't stay longer. We had a lovely time last night, so there! We stayed awake for hours talking. She told me every single thing she did while she was up in Grafton and then she showed me how you do sloping satin-stitch properly and then she recited this poem she learned in elocution. And . . . Oh, geeze, give me a break! Take that little Goody Two-Shoes off my hands and down to the park! She's driving me nuts! Tell you what, I'll let you wear my coral bangle to school one day each . . .'

'Viv and I had other plans for today,' Cathy said. 'We were going down to Isobel's to practise for the Christmas concert she's putting on in her garage to raise money for the Red Cross.'

'Well, you could take Rita with you. She could recite "The Lady of Shalott".'

'I love that poem,' Vivienne said. 'Specially that line that goes "All in the blue unclouded weather" – it's like summer here in Wilgawa.'

'You wouldn't still like it if you'd heard Rita recite it forty thousand times!'

'There wouldn't be any point taking her with us, because Isobel's concert's not on till next month and Rita's going home tonight. Thank goodness. Besides, you did say we weren't allowed to bother you both while she's here.'

'The loan of my coral bangle plus sixpence each and I won't tell Mum how you ripped up the mosquito net to play "Bride of Dracula" with. Come on, don't be so mean! I'll shout you both a double-header ice-cream next time the van comes around. Oh, I couldn't stand being lumbered with Miss Perfect all day! You wouldn't believe how gruesome it was last night! When she finally got through "The Lady of Shalott" and we turned out the light, she wanted a drink of water. I got up and fetched her one, only the tap water was full of wrigglers and I didn't notice, but she certainly did! Then she was cold and wanted another quilt. It was so embarrassing, all I could find was that dreadful old army blanket of Dad's. You know, that one all riddled with holes where he said the enemy crept into the trenches and tried to bayonet him to death.'

'Only Mum reckons they're just moth-holes,' Cathy said. 'Bet a certain person doesn't have moth-holey blankets at her house!'

'She doesn't have an embarrassing father, either! This morning was just awful! He got up at the crack of dawn and lit the kitchen fire swearing his head off because the wood was all green. Rita was sitting up in bed listening to every word with her ears out like aerodrome windsocks. They stuck out even more when he started singing that awful version of "Roll Out the Barrel" Mum always goes mad at him for. Then the cow wouldn't come for milking so he saddled up Digger and tore around the paddock cracking his stockwhip and yelling and drove her in the bail that way. I told Rita we had this peculiar old man who comes in to help with the milking in the morning and it was only him, but I don't think she believed me. Oh, I don't want to be landed with her all to myself today!'

But it was taken out of her hands. 'Come on, you hussies!' Dad roared over the veranda rail. 'Out of those beds and look lively! I've put some beaut tucker together and the horses in the buggy all rearing to go. We're taking that nice little girl of Elsie's up the river for a picnic.'

Heather rushed into the kitchen and whispered furiously, 'Mum, can't you do anything? I'll die if we have to go out in that buggy! No one else in town has one any more – what's Rita going to think?'

'Don't be so snobby, Heather,' Mum said. 'A picnic and a swim on a sunny day like this would be nice and I'm only sorry I don't have time to go along, but I'm making some doyley pressers.'

'Doyley pressers?'

'Just an idea I had. Those records that got scratched when Dad threw them at the flying foxes in the peach tree – I thought I could stick bits of broken china all over them, then bore a couple of hinge holes with a hot skewer and thread them up with ribbon. To keep doyleys flat in – I think it would look pretty.'

'It would look just as mad as the ping-pong ball curtain! Oh Mum, I don't want to go out with *him*!'

'Rita will enjoy seeing the pretty countryside around here. It's very good of your father to offer to take you all out, so hurry up and get ready and don't keep him waiting.'

'A buggy . . .' Rita said uncertainly, gazing at it. 'How . . . quaint.'

Heather treacherously left her to sit on the front seat all alone with Dad while she squeezed in the back next to Cathy and Vivienne. But instead of turning right, he headed towards town.

'Where are we going?' Cathy demanded. 'I thought we were driving up river for a swim and a picnic . . .'

'Elsie's girl would like to see the War Memorial first,' Dad said, as though it were beyond all possible doubt. Heather folded up like a concertina, trying to hide from the crowds of people coming out of early Mass at Saint Joseph's on Tavistell Street. Isobel, resplendent amongst them in a moon-sized beret she'd decorated with a rhinestone butterfly, waved cheekily and called out, 'Hey, Uncle

Leighton, watch out for Injuns!' Dad growled deep down in his throat at the sight of her, but when they reached the War Memorial he took off his ancient, treasured slouch-hat and held it reverently over his heart, standing upright in the buggy for a three-minute silence.

'It's not Anzac Day or anything,' Heather told Rita, who was looking very puzzled. 'He just likes war things. Sometimes he takes his hat off in front of the Town Hall cannon, too. That's how he got his gammy leg, in the war before this last one.'

'Though sometimes he says he got a bullet in it, and sometimes it's shrapnel and other times a bayonet,' Cathy explained. 'Only Mum reckons what really happened is he kicked a camel – he's sort of got a bad temper – and the camel kicked him right back. Mum and Dad met through the war. She knitted things for the soldiers and she put her photo and address in the toe of a sock. And Dad thought she was so pretty – she wasn't fat in those olden days – he sent a photo of himself back.'

'You should see it,' Vivienne said. 'He's got this funny moustache all waxed at the tips and he's leaning against an Egyptian tomb – or at least that's what he said it was. Only Mum found out later it was just an army mess hall in Sydney before he even left for overseas with the Light Horse Brigade . . .'

'What's all that nattering in the back?' Dad said angrily, ending his three-minute silence. Before he put his hat back on he turned around and cuffed them all with it. 'Not an ounce of respect for the fallen!' he scolded. 'Can't even hold your waggy tongues for a couple of minutes! You want to follow this young miss's good example – she knows how to sit quiet and show proper respect where it's due!'

It was obvious that he'd taken quite a shine to Rita. He gave her his full attention on the long drive up the river into the foothills, telling her about the time he'd accidentally side-swiped a huge goanna on this very stretch of road, and how it had flicked upwards and landed in his lap, and then jumped out onto Digger's back and both horses had bolted. Rita clutched the buggy armrest and kept peering down at the road a lot. She'd turned rather pale under the straw sun-hat she claimed she always wore in summer to stop herself getting horrible orange freckles. Heather, who had more freckles than anyone in Wilgawa, had thought that an extremely tactless remark. She felt even more annoyed because the only time Dad paid any attention to her during the drive was when he spied something worth stealing in a field they passed. 'Look at that – a roll of good fencing wire just left lying around!' he marvelled, reining in the horses. 'Out you hop . . . you – Vivienne, Cathy, Grace, can't remember your name . . .'

'Heather,' Heather said sulkily. 'And I'm not nipping under that fence to pinch some rusty old wire! What if the farmer sees me?'

'Have a bit of gumption – just pretend you've gone in there to do a tinkle if anyone comes,' Dad said. 'Grab one of those watermelons, too, while you're about it.'

When she'd got back and the melon and wire were stowed away under Rita's disapproving feet, he took a short cut to the picnic spot, plunging without warning down a steep little gully. He took off his hat and waved it around his head, whooping, until they landed safely at the bottom in a hurricane of red dust and pebbles. Rita had been too terrified to make a sound, but Heather and Cathy and Vivienne, picking themselves up from the floor of the buggy, stormed at Dad that they'd tell Mum on him the moment they got home.

'Pack of squalling sissies!' he said disgustedly. 'Not a peep out of this one in the front, though – she's made of the right metal!'

'I'm never never *never* coming out with him again!' Heather vowed after they'd changed into bathing costumes and were dunking themselves in the river to get rid of the red dust.

But Vivienne thought that it was worth it, once you'd actually arrived in one piece. The river here was a drowsy, gentle thing, crooning to itself in a cradle of willow fronds. The water was so clear the coloured pebbles on the bed were like jewels under glass, and shallow enough to wade right over to the other side. Rita, she noticed, had done exactly that, probably to get as far away from Dad as she could, but he didn't even notice he was being snubbed. He lit a fire between some flat stones and boiled the billy, throwing in great handfuls of tea and a few gum leaves so that the tea would come out as black as a dog's nose and so bitter no one else would drink it, which was just as he liked it.

'We'd better go over and talk to Rita. We've got to entertain her, I suppose,' Heather said reluctantly, so they crossed over to where she stood waist-high in the water, looking as though she wasn't enjoying herself very much.

'Want to have a race down to the next bend?' Heather asked. 'Or we could practise life-saving. I'm going for my life-saver's badge in Guides soon.'

'I already got mine ages ago,' Rita said.

'Do you want to sail leaf boats?' Vivienne said. 'We each get a different coloured leaf and put them in the current and the first one to reach the little island wins.'

'Do you want to skim stones over the water?' Cathy suggested when Rita shook her head. 'Dad's really good at that, he can make them skip about five times. Or there's this other game – you pretend to be enemy submarines and he runs up and down the bank and chucks bombs out and you have to dodge. It's quite safe – the bombs are only horse dollops, really.'

'I don't think so, thanks,' Rita said.

'You'll get your shoulders all sunburnt if you just stand there doing nothing,' Heather said tersely. 'Come on down the river a bit, there's this lovely deep pool all edged with boulders. I can nearly duck-dive right down to the bottom of it.'

'I can dive properly, I already learned at the city baths,' Rita said, and went downstream and took over the rock pool completely, showing off. They watched her jealously.

'Pity you've got to go back on the train tonight,' Cathy lied. 'It's a shame it's just a drop-in visit on your way back from Grafton. If you'd stayed longer we could have all gone to the beach.'

'Oh, I can walk to three different beaches any old time from where I live,' Rita bragged. 'I get bored with them really. Why's Vivienne just sitting there on the bank? Why doesn't she come into the deep part?'

'Because she's a sook,' Cathy said unkindly. 'She can't even dog-paddle yet, even though she's ten. I don't know how anyone can be so babyish for their age. She sent away for these stupid magic beans advertised in the kiddy pages of a magazine. And when they came in the mail and they didn't work, she blubbed like anything!'

Vivienne blushed. That advertisement had pictured a beautiful turreted castle, and if you sent a postal note for two shillings and sixpence, you'd receive six magic beans like the ones Jack had planted. That two-and-six had meant weeks of running messages, taking bottles back to the shop and bartering all her treasures with Heather and Cathy. But when the beans arrived, they'd just been ugly little mottled plaster pellets. She'd had a vision of pearly objects that would glow as soon as she took them into her hand, and still remembered her anguish.

'Hey, look – there's something shining at the bottom of the pool,' Cathy said, and thankfully they all stopped smirking at Vivienne's red face and dived. Rita got there first and came up with a metal button.

'It's got a little eagle printed on it,' she said. Vivienne asked to see, but Rita said meanly that she wouldn't show it to anyone who was too sooky to put their head underwater and believed in magic beans.

Vivienne forlornly took herself off. She went and watched Dad getting the picnic ready, even though she thought it looked terrible. He'd opened a tin of camp-pie and dumped thick slabs on to even thicker slices of bread. There was the stolen watermelon hacked into chunks and he'd brought along a cold plum pudding left over from last Christmas. He liked making the plum puddings every Christmas, but didn't follow any recipe and added peculiar things, so they tended to sit around from one December to the next, uneaten.

'It doesn't look very dainty,' Vivienne said critically. 'Heather should have made some nice little sandwiches, seeing that girl's her special visitor. And we should have a tablecloth spread out on the grass, not just the food dumped down like that on the stump of a tree. Proper picnics have chicken drumsticks and salad with the cucumber all sliced up thin . . . There's ants getting into the sugar, Dad.'

'Flaming little snob, turning your nose up at good tucker!' Dad said. 'We never got lovely tucker like this in the trenches, I can tell you! That other girl, Elsie's one – she's got more sense. She won't grizzle about wanting roast chicken and namby-pamby salad and cream cakes. Bet you won't catch her turning up her nose at good grub like this!'

Rita didn't. She was too much in awe of Dad. Wrapped in a towel, she sat on a log and nibbled her huge camp-pie sandwich, while the others fed theirs stealthily to a family of kookaburras. She even ate a slice of the revolting cold plum pudding, which was as hard and indigestible as slate. Heather and Cathy and Vivienne flatly refused to eat any of it, though Dad called them a whole string of names and compared them unflatteringly to Rita. But he was in a fairly benign mood and even joined in a game of 'Old Witch' with them. He made a superlative Old Witch. Every time he spun around to catch anyone in the act of moving, he put on a different blood-curdling face, and Rita was too alarmed to even budge from the starting line. Dad said that she'd won every game and gave her sixpence.

'That's not fair!' Cathy yelled. 'She didn't even join in . . .'

'Quit your squawking,' Dad said crossly, bored now with the game. 'Go on, clear out! Bunch of blathering flibbertigibbets, can't a man get any peace?' He stomped off to fossick about among the little gullies, splitting open stones to examine each one thoughtfully, so they all went in for another swim until the shadows had crept right over to the other side of the river.

'Dad, we'd better get a move on back home,' Heather said. 'Rita has to be on the eight o'clock train.'

Dad, who wouldn't have hurried himself for anyone else, went and unhobbled the horses, which had stopped grazing and were resting gently side by side, each whisking flies from the other with its tail. 'Had a good swim, Missy?' he boomed at Rita as she climbed unwillingly into the buggy, and she jumped and dropped the bright button she'd found. Dad picked it up and looked at it.

'She found it in that pool near the boulders,' Cathy explained. 'Even though I really saw it first . . .'

'I'll be blowed!' Dad said. 'Well, I reckon it's off a poor old swaggy I found in there a year back. He was wearing a checky shirt with buttons like this one. Poor old codger, must've been on the metho and toppled in, been in the river a couple of months by the look of him – his face was all et away by eels.'

'A dead body in that pool where we were swimming? Where I put my face under the water?' Rita squeaked, and lost her plum pudding and camp-pie quietly over the buggy wheel.

Heather, Cathy and Vivienne thought that would be the end of Dad's unqualified admiration. Usually he despised people who threw up, believing they only did it to call attention to themselves and show off. But now he made them all squeeze up in the front seat of the buggy on the way home so Rita could have the back part all to herself to lie down if she felt like it.

'Sensitive little girl, that,' he said. 'Real nice and ladylike. Pity all you gabby baggages don't take a leaf out of her copy-book.'

He seemed genuinely sorry that Rita was leaving that night, though everyone else could hardly wait to get rid of her. Rita looked as though she could hardly wait to leave, for that matter. As soon as they got back from the picnic, she dived inside and started to pack, then sat on her suitcase by the front door, even though it wasn't nearly time to leave for the train. She kept peeping anxiously at the little gold wrist-watch with Roman numerals she'd been given last year for coming top in something or other at school.

'You'd better eat something, love,' Mum said. 'You've got that long trip ahead of you.'

'No thanks, Aunty Connie. I'm not all that hungry.'

'Then let me make you a packet of sandwiches. And I could cut some slices of plum pudding . . .'

'I'm truly not hungry,' Rita said. 'Er . . . you did say we'd be getting a taxi down to the station, didn't you?'

'Yes, that's right. Old Digger will be tired after the long drive up river, so Dad won't want to harness him up again today. If the taxi's not here by ten-past seven, Heather will run up to the hospital phone box and ask Mr Truran to get a move on, so there's nothing to worry about. It's such a shame you can't stay longer, dear, but I dare say you'll be able to come again some other time.'

'Well, I don't know,' Rita said evasively. 'It's hard to fit things in with my elocution lessons and all that.'

'Good luck with your reciting in the eisteddfod,' said Heather, watching the mantel clock.

'I'll write and tell you about it when I win first prize,' said Rita.

'Oh yes, we must keep up our letters,' said Heather, secretly thinking that she'd toss the chocolate box crammed with all the years of Rita's dull, egocentric, boring letters into the kitchen fire and never write her another line.

Cathy and Vivienne yawned behind their hands, listening impatiently for any sound of a taxi stopping at the gate. As soon as Rita was off, they thought, they could take all their bedding back into the bedroom. And tonight Heather would be so glad to be rid of that tiresome Rita, she'd read them the next instalment of the spine-chilling, glorious serial she was writing about how Mr O'Keefe had secretly been married to twenty different brides and murdered each one and dumped their bodies in a quarry at the brickworks.

'You'll be able to get a lot of fancywork done on the train trip,' Mum said into the unamiable silence. 'Er . . . Heather, maybe you'd better run up now and remind Mr Truran about the taxi we ordered . . .'

'Taxi?' Dad said, crashing noisily in at the back door. 'What's this frittering money on taxis?'

'Oh, please don't go to the bother of harnessing up the horses again, Uncle Leighton!' Rita begged, and looked as though she might cry. 'I can *walk* down to the station, really I can! My suitcase isn't all that heavy . . .'

'What a nice polite little girl,' Dad said admiringly. 'Not like these lazy, loud-mouthed trollops. But I've got good news for you, Missy. Just been up to the hospital phone and I got on to your silly old chook of a mother and asked if you could stay another couple of days. It's not right, I told her, that you've got to go off so soon. So she said you can stay till next weekend, how about that, eh? Aren't you pleased, you girls? Tomorrow we can show Elsie's girl all over my tung-oil nut plantation!'

The Best-Looking House in Town

The best-looking house in town was white and surrounded by velvety lawn, sown from special grass seed. You couldn't see into the backyard because the side paths were blocked with tall red gates. Elegantly festooned blinds screened the front windows. Curly pillars like barley-sugar sticks supported the porch, and the roof tiles were the colour of tomato sauce and lapped over each other like little tongues. The house lay on the river side of the road, so Vivienne always took a seat on that side of the bus for the intense pleasure of being able to have a good stare twice a day. The school bus stopped almost exactly in front of it. All the kids who came over by the ferry had to be picked up and put down there, and so did Marjorie Powell. She didn't use the ferry, she lived in the beautiful Spanish house.

Occasionally Marjorie would be running late and Vivienne nearly dislocated her neck trying to peer inside the house while the front door was open. But all she ever saw was Mrs Powell handing over a wrapped school lunch or a forgotten pencil-box. Marjorie never hurried herself when she was late, as though she expected the whole world, including buses, to wait about for her. She would just plod solidly across the road in her pretty dress, and not even offer the driver an excuse as she handed over her fare.

Vivienne stared at the Powell house so often and so intently that she could have drawn it from memory with no mistakes. The letter-box was like a miniature house itself, complete with a red tiled roof. There were six little cypress trees like green blades planted three on either side of the porch, and the front garden looked so glorious that Vivienne fancied the back garden must be just as splendid. It was a pity the side gates kept it hidden from view. Probably the lawn at the back ran all the way down to the river, and there could even be a little pier with a boat moored to a barley-sugar pole, just like the ones by the porch. Perhaps something as fantastic as a gondola. And there'd be an iron-lace gazebo, winding paths with archways and a fountain.

If the back garden was like that, the inside of the house must be truly magnificent! Once she'd sat near two ladies on the bus when it passed the Powell house, and one had said, 'My word, that house is a real palace!' The closest thing Vivienne could imagine to a palace was the upper floor of the Roxy picture theatre in town. When she went to a matinee it was always the cheap seats downstairs, but a few times she'd sneaked upstairs into the posh expensive part when the usherette wasn't looking. Ruby Feltex carpeting, little gold harp-shaped chairs with velvet seats, rich curtains looped back with gold tasselled ropes . . . the Powell house would look exactly like that inside.

She was so besotted by the house that she wove fantasies about how she could get herself invited inside. For instance, it might happen that the chimney caught fire. She would leap out through the bus window, fill her school-case with water from the front tap, scramble up on the roof and douse that fire all by herself. Mrs Powell would be so grateful she'd invite her to stay for a week in a guest-room panelled in mauve brocade with a chandelier. Or she'd be walking by the river and hear a pathetic cry for help – Marjorie drowning from cramp. She'd jump in with no thought for her own safety, tow Marjorie ashore and apply resuscitation. Then Mr Powell would appear – perhaps he'd been fishing further along the river and hadn't heard Marjorie fall in – and insist that Vivienne come back to the house for afternoon tea. They'd all walk up through the incredibly beautiful back garden, only just when they reached the house she'd collapse (she could have injured her back hauling Marjorie out of the water) which would mean a long stay in the Powell house till she recovered.

One afternoon when the sun was so energetic it made the white house shimmer like a mirage, she just couldn't help herself. She got off impetuously at the ferry bus-stop. The bus moved on and Marjorie went in at her gate, while the ferry kids eyed Vivienne. 'What d'you think you're up to, getting off here?' they demanded, and Marjorie heard and looked back.

'Nothing. I mean . . . I have to . . . have to deliver a message to someone,' Vivienne said uneasily, because she was scared of those tough dairy-farm kids from over the river. They helped milk dozens of cows before school so that they often fell asleep at their desks, but underneath their doziness they were a formidable, united army. They stood in front of her like a thorny hedge, blocking the footpath. One of them grabbed her plaits and pretended she was a plough-horse and another tweaked the hem of her skirt and yelped, 'We can see yer bloomers!'

'I'll t-tell on you!' Vivienne stammered and they rampaged down to the ferry screeching insults, but they only went because the ferry was coming across. Vivienne retrieved her dropped school-bag and walked as slowly as she could up the footpath, inspecting the best-looking house in town at close range. There was a beautiful iridescent vase like a tulip on a window ledge; a Spanish dancing doll on another . . .

'Hey!' said Marjorie, still standing in her gateway. Vivienne stopped and offered her friendliest smile. Even though Marjorie was in a higher class at school and had never before acknowledged her existence, perhaps she felt sorry that Vivienne had been picked on like that by the ferry kids. Maybe she'd invite her in and offer her lemonade and lamingtons snowy with coconut . . . 'Cut out that sticky-beaking over the fence at our house!' Marjorie said.

'I wasn't! I only got off here to visit my cousin . . .'

'Your cousin's that peculiar Isobel Dion and she certainly doesn't live anywhere around here,' Marjorie said.

Vivienne peered avidly over her shoulder at the house, gleaning information. There was a fancy grid by the front door for scraping shoes and a porch lamp almost as impressive as the one carried by the Statue of Liberty. 'I didn't mean Isobel, I meant this other cousin I've got in Wilgawa, second cousin, really,' she lied. 'What's . . . what's your back garden like?'

Marjorie's eyes narrowed suspiciously.

'Your front yard's so lovely, I just wondered . . .'

'It's even nicer round the back,' Marjorie said. 'That's why we keep it locked up so rubbernecks like you can't see in. I've got a double-storey playhouse out there.'

'Oh!' said Vivienne. 'A double-storey playhouse!'

'And there's arches and a wishing-well and statues so big you've got to get up on a ladder to clean the moss of their faces.'

'Oooh!' said Vivienne. 'Could you . . . can't you open the side gate so I can have a quick look?'

Marjorie eyed her scornfully from head to toe and when she got to Vivienne's feet she said, 'You've got your sister Cathy's sandals on. Do you share the shoes in your family, then?'

'We don't! They're not! We both have matching pairs . . .'

'Cathy had those exact same ones on at school yesterday. The buckle's come off and someone's sewn it back on with blue wool, so that's how I know. Anyway, they're miles too big for you, so you needn't pretend, you little squirt. Erk – fancy having to wear shoes someone else's feet have been in! Now – get lost and don't let me catch you hanging around our house ever again!'

Vivienne walked home, humiliated. It was a long walk and unfortunate things happened to her all the way. The Sylvesters' evil-tempered fox terrier rushed, growling, out of a driveway. She was scared of all dogs except Dad's old Bluey, and crossed quickly to the other side of the street. The terrier chased after her so she had to zigzag nimbly until it gave up and went back to lurk about for another target. Then the buckle of Cathy's sandal came right off, so she had to walk barefoot and trod on a prickle. While she was getting it out, boring old Mrs Farrer popped her head over the fence to start a conversation. Vivienne, a fly caught in a web of rambling vocalised memories, couldn't get away for ten minutes. Then Stewart Thurlow chased her all the way up the hospital hill pelting her with bullet-hard green plums, and when she finally got home, Cathy sang out triumphantly, 'Here she is! Told you she got off the bus at the ferry-crossing and walked home!'

Mum was in one of her martyred, peppery-tempered moods and wasn't impressed by Vivienne's complex lie about having to draw a picture of the ferry for school.

'You girls know very well you're to come straight home!' Mum scolded. 'Not only do I have to put up with your father, but I work my fingers to the bone for the whole lot of you and get no help whatsoever! From dawn to midnight it's slave slave slave, and what thanks do I get?'

Vivienne glanced cynically around at the untidy room, then at the stack of papers by the typewriter.

'Gallivanting around town instead of coming home to give me a hand . . . I'd like to know when I ever get the chance to amble by the river watching the ferry!'

'Just about every day and weekends, too, if you didn't spend so much time over that poetry. Anyway, Heather and Grace do most of the housework,' Vivienne muttered sulkily but took care not to be overheard. Mum, in one of those rare moods, was as scary as Hitler. And as for that tattle-tale Cathy – but the only retribution she could think of for the moment was to sew the sandal buckle back on using a thread with no knot at the start. It was Cathy's turn to wear them to school tomorrow, while she wore the detested white lace-ups that Grace, Heather and Cathy had all worn to Sunday School over the years. They were too tight and and nipped at your heels like the Sylvesters' fox terrier. Oh, how she'd love a pair of new shoes unworn by anyone else, bought specially for her alone! But there was no likelihood of that ever happening. She bit the thread off and looked at the sandal with satisfaction. That buckle might just hold out till playtime tomorrow, but not much longer.

Next day, however, she had troubles of her own, and they started as soon as Marjorie Powell got on at the ferry-crossing bus-stop. 'What do you reckon you're doing in *my* seat, Vivienne Melling?' Marjorie said. 'I always sit there. Move!'

'But . . . you usually sit up the front behind Mr Kelt,' Vivienne protested.

'I sit in a whole lot of different places and I don't want to find them all cluttered up with teeny little wet-the-bed 5B kids, either!'

Vivienne looked over her shoulder at Cathy further down the bus, but Cathy was scribbling hasty homework and hadn't noticed anything. She glanced speculatively at Stewart Thurlow across the aisle. He liked fights so much he'd often join in ones that weren't any of his business, but the trouble was you couldn't be sure which side he'd choose. So she moved cravenly to a seat further along. Marjorie looked sated with power, as though she had a booted foot on someone's neck and a dripping sword in one hand. She must have enjoyed feeling so powerful, because at lunch break, when Vivienne was queuing to get a drink of water at the taps, she charged up and said, 'Just who do you think you are, shoving to the front of the line like that?'

'Did not! I never . . .'

'Oh yes you did, I was watching! Nancy was ahead of you but you sneaked in front when she wasn't looking. Isn't that right, Nance?'

'I don't . . .' Nancy Tuckett whispered.

'See, Nancy's not going to be pushed around like that. You let her have her proper turn, or she'll go over to the office and tell Mr P. on you!'

It just wasn't fair, Vivienne thought angrily as she gave up her place at the tap, that such an obnoxious bully should live in the best house in town. And when they were on the bus going home, Marjorie still kept up the bullying. Vivienne received a note with her name on it passed along the aisle. Inside was a drawing of a giant-sized Roman sandal and crowded into the sandal was a whole mob of raggedy-looking kids. Vivienne, who was sensitive about the lack of new clothes in her family and all the handing down and doing without, blushed the same colour as her hair. But Marjorie's nastiness didn't stop her gazing admiringly at the sparkling Powell house when the bus stopped at the ferry-crossing.

Marjorie, pleased with her victim, thought up other forms of persecution during the week. Cathy found Vivienne hiding in the toilets because she was too scared to go out in the playground. But she wasn't very sympathetic and only said, 'Just stay away from Marjorie Powell. She's nasty, she can get people saying horrible things they don't really mean. I used to hang around with her myself a few weeks ago till I learned better.'

'Make her stop picking on me,' Vivienne pleaded. 'She gave me a Chinese burn in Assembly. She told all the kids in my class we're related to the Gathins and she reckoned Mum made my Sunday School dress out of an old flour bag . . . go and sock her, Cathy!'

'Sock her yourself,' Cathy said unhelpfully. 'It's got nothing to do with me. Everyone crawls like mad hoping they'll get invited to her posh house, but she never asks anyone, she's too stuck up. Well, it's no skin off my nose. I just ignore her now.'

Vivienne got through the days somehow and consoled

herself at the weekend by making a model of the Powells' back garden. She created miniature paths with river pebbles and a summer-house from twigs laced together. The lawns were moss prised from under the water-tank and there was even a plasticine peacock studded with broken green-glass marbles. She played with it all Saturday and again on Sunday morning, because Cathy and Heather were off on business of their own and wouldn't let her join in.

'Viv,' Mum called. 'Can you think up a rhyme that goes with "for ever"? I'm writing a little verse for the Hawke girl's engagement – what do you think of this . . .

'"*O, radiant young couple, to be united in joy,*
I hope your shining love will last for ever!
Throughout the stormy gales of life's great sorrows,
And also . . ."'

'"And also in the blue unclouded weather,"' Vivienne said obligingly. 'Mum, can I have that little broken mirror from your purse? I want to make a lily-pond.'

'Yes, love, of course you can. Oh, that's truly beautiful, that rhyme you made up! I'm going to type the whole verse on a card and paint a little border of violets. Here's the mirror . . . and oh dear, there's a message here in my purse I forgot all about. It's from your dad to the sawmill about bits and pieces of timber he's going to need next week, so you'd better take it across now.'

'It's Sunday,' Vivienne said. 'The sawmill's closed on Sundays.'

'Oh, is it really Sunday?' Mum asked vaguely. 'I thought it must be a school day, the house is so quiet. Oh drat, then! Your father's not going to be pleased when he comes home from up river and finds this message hasn't been sent. He makes as much din as a tornado when he's cross, even though he's not what you'd call a powerfully built man.'

'Isobel reckons he looks like one of his tung-oil nuts,' Vivienne said. 'All bark and no bite.'

'Then Isobel's a very rude, cheeky girl talking about her uncle like that! Your dad's very nice looking, even if he isn't all that tall. He looks just like Errol Flynn in his old army photo, so you can tell Isobel to put that in her pipe and smoke it!'

'She only smokes roll-your-own cigarettes,' Vivienne said, but Mum was frowning distractedly at the note.

'I know – you could take it down to Mr Powell at his house.'

'To the Powell house?' Vivienne cried with delight.

That meant she could go right up to the front door and knock, and Marjorie couldn't do a thing about it! When they opened the door she'd be able to get a proper look inside that palace, be able to see the marble floors and the little gold harp-shaped chairs covered in velvet . . .

'Don't drop the note on the way. Oh, and coming home you can get a packet of tea and a loaf of bread and some mutton chops . . .'

'Shops are shut, Mum,' Vivienne said.

'Are they? How silly, shutting them on a week day,' said Mum, going back to her typewriter.

Vivienne went and tidied herself. It seemed fitting, when she'd actually been given licence to walk up the front path of the best-looking house in town and knock on its magical front door. She borrowed Heather's embroidered peasant blouse and Cathy's clean socks, even though she knew vengeance would be extracted later, then set off down the river road. Mrs Farrer was gazing wistfully over her fence for someone to talk to, but Vivienne said, 'I'm sorry I can't stop, Mrs Farrer. I've got to take a message to the Powell house.'

'The Powells . . .' Mrs Farrer said. 'Let's see, she was one of the Atkinson girls before she married Reg Powell, and the Atkinsons originally came from Birramudgee . . .' but Vivienne flew past, holding the note as reverently as though it were a golden key. She didn't even worry about Sylvester's terrier, but just said as authoritatively as Heather or Cathy would have, 'You! Gerrout! Get home!' and it yipped once without conviction and scooted back behind the hedge.

When she reached the Powell house she stood on the pavement and drew a deep breath, savouring every moment, because this might never happen again. She unlatched the low gate, which swung open on well-oiled hinges, and hoped that the occupants of a passing car would think that *she* lived here, in the glorious palace. The metal toe and heel protectors on the soles of her white shoes clacked on the red-brick drive, and she walked as slowly as possible, enjoying the sound even though she hated the shoes themselves. She went up the three steps to the porch and looked at the smart front door. It was painted red to match the gates and had a brass knocker set in the middle. She knocked three times, then stood on the mat wearing a winsome expression, so that Mrs Powell, when she opened the door, would know she was a nicely brought-up little girl and perhaps ask her inside out of the heat while the note was read.

But no one answered. She knocked many times and

waited, and the brightness seemed to leach out of the morning. Her disappointment became as hard to bear as the time she'd been in the infants' school and Mum had made her an incredibly beautiful crepe-paper bonnet to wear for a fancy-hat parade. She'd taken that bonnet to school the day beforehand to show the teacher, but next day, the day of the parade, she'd been away sick and the teacher had let Joyce Sylvester wear it in the parade instead. And Joyce won first prize, a bag of lollies, but she'd gobbled them all up and not saved any for Vivienne.

This was just as unfair, the Powells being out! Even if Mr Powell had grumbled at her for bothering him with sawmill business on a Sunday, it would have been worth it. The door would have to be open while he was doing the grumbling, and she could have peered into the hall.

Perhaps the Powells were all out the back and hadn't heard her knocking! That was even better – now she could see the magnificent back garden! She jumped off the porch, ran past the little spear-shaped trees and opened the latch of the left-hand gate. Fountains, she thought blissfully. Ferneries, lawns stretching down to the river, a double-storey playhouse and statues so tall you had to wash their faces from a ladder . . .

She shut her eyes, stepped through the gate as though entering Camelot, then slowly opened her eyes and looked around at . . . the messiest, ugliest jumble she'd ever seen in her life! Timber was stacked everywhere, great untidy piles of it, and machinery – rusting old car bodies and tractors! She had a quick memory of her dad saying that Mr Powell was a mean old cuss and never threw away a thing in his life if he could possibly help it . . .

She edged through a maze of smelly lino rolls, caches

of empty bottles and great coils of rusted barbed wire, looking desperately past them for lawns and lily-ponds. But the maze led straight to the porch at the back of the palace. And it wasn't a palace, not out here! The back of the house was just an ordinary shabby fibro cottage with corrugated iron roofing! It was only a sham, that part out the front – like the stage scenery in Isobel's last dancing-school concert, which was painted to look like a temple on one side, but the other was just raw plywood with the stencilled words, 'Wilgawa Butter Factory'!

As for the garden – there wasn't one; just Mrs Powell's washing lines and a fowl-run with some dispirited-looking chooks pecking around in a pumpkin vine. No rose arbours, no lily ponds, and as for Marjorie's double-storey playhouse – that was just a couple of old wooden boxes nailed up in a tree with a bit of broken ladder for steps! Cathy and Heather could make better tree-houses wearing blindfolds!

It couldn't possibly be true – there must be at least one beautiful thing to salvage from her dream! She forced a way through the pumpkin vine to the river, but found no pier, no moored gondola. You couldn't even get down the bank to the water's edge, because Mr Powell had put up a hideous barbed wire fence!

Vivienne went back to the rickety forgery of a house and knocked sternly on the kitchen door, but no one came. She went back out the front, slamming the side gate behind her, and shoved the note in the letter-box. She could have bellowed from the immensity of her disappointment. It was nearly as bad as when she'd got half-way through reading *Anne of Green Gables* at Isobel's place. Isobel wouldn't ever let her take it home, so she'd had to snatch reading sessions while visiting. And one day Isobel had said casually, 'Oh, that old book . . . too bad, I didn't know you hadn't finished it yet. I swapped it with a girl at school for a snake bangle.' Or the time at the matinee interval when lucky seat numbers were called out for kids to go up on the stage to get a mystery present, and she'd heard the man say 'Forty-nine' and rushed excitedly forward, but it had been seat number forty-five.

She shut the front gate and turned sadly away. And came face to face with Marjorie Powell strutting home all tricked out in her best dress with a big white ribbon perched on top of her curls like a pigeon.

'What are you doing at our letter-box?' Marjorie demanded. 'I saw you put something in there!'

'It's only a message for your dad,' Vivienne said. 'It was about timber. I knocked on the front door . . .'

'You've got a nerve knocking on our front door! Mum and Dad are out, anyhow. If you had a message, you should have taken it up to the sawmill like everyone else. What a cheek! Go on, shove off! I'm going in to get changed, then I'm going to have a swim in the river. No one else is allowed to use the river behind our back garden, it's reserved. We've got a diving board there and a trapeze swing that goes right out over the water.'

'Have you?' said Vivienne.

'Just told you so, didn't I? Go on, get out of the way – this part of the footpath's reserved, too, same as our part of the river. After my swim I'm going to play in my double-storey playhouse. It's got real electric light in it.'

'Has it?' asked Vivienne.

'You deaf or something? Just said so, didn't I? You want to wash your ears out.'

'No one came to your front door so . . . I've just been

round to the back one. Right inside your backyard.'

It was funny about Marjorie's eyes, Vivienne thought. Usually you could never meet that blazing blue stare, as overpowering as the stream of sparks from a welding torch. But now something was happening to that stare. It flickered confusedly, then vanished completely under sandy lashes lowered in embarrassment. And Marjorie suddenly hurried up the front path, tripped over the mat in her confusion, and let herself in through the door, not even looking back. Vivienne turned away from the best-looking house in town and didn't look back, either.

Miracle

'It's going to be a fruit-cake with almond icing on top,' Cathy said. 'Mum's going to bake it soon as she gets back from town, but we probably won't ever get any. It's being put aside for Eleanor Grantby's visit.'

'Four whole eggs,' said Isobel respectfully. 'My mum never uses more than two for a cake.'

'Eleanor Grantby's kind of special,' said Cathy. 'She's that stuck-up thing who lives on a big property up the river, used to board in town with the Sylvesters' when she was at high school. Grace and her were in the same class, and she's coming here to stay while they make their debut together. It's still three weeks off, but you should see the way Grace is carrying on! She's already got Mum chasing all over town buying proper cups and saucers that match and a guest-towel and some serviettes.'

'Why don't we make the cake and have it all ready as a surprise when your mum gets back?'

'But I've never baked anything much before, only rock-cakes. And no one would eat them, so we threw them out to the chooks, but they didn't fancy them, either. Mum tried to paint one and use it for a paperweight!'

'Fruit-cake shouldn't be all that difficult. It's just the same as an ordinary one, only you chuck in raisins and sultanas and lemon peel . . .'

'Isobel, I don't think we'd better. That oven's a cow of a thing and Mum's the only one who knows when it's hot enough for baking. These are the very last eggs, too.'

'But I *want* to do it. It's part of my vocation to act kind to someone every day from now on. There's a Mission on at our church and Sister's been making us go to early Mass every morning and Benediction at night, too, but I'm glad now she did. It's how I discovered my vocation.'

'What's a vocation?'

'Kind of something holy you're going to do with your life.'

'Holy? I thought you were going to Hollywood and be in films . . .'

'All that Hollywood business was a mistake. The first day the Mission started, Father Cassidy – you should see him, Cathy, he looks just like Gary Cooper, no kidding! – visited all the class-rooms and he seemed to be looking at me directly with these piercing blue eyes. That's when I realised. I'm not going to be a film starlet any more when I leave school. I'm going to be – a nun!'

'But . . . that would mean you couldn't ever have a perm, and you'd have to give up tap-dancing! Honest, Isobel, I just can't see . . .'

'Doesn't matter. I'm going to give up everything and mortify my flesh. I've got such a strong vocation I wouldn't be at all surprised if I ended up doing miracles and being made a saint! Father Cassidy – he's got one of those Kirk Douglas chins with a cleft in it – was saying everyone could be saints if they tried. He reckons every little act of kindness counts, every kind word and thought and deed.'

'Like in Girl Guides?'

'It's not a bit like Girl Guides! Geeze, it's a crying shame your side of the family never stuck to the Faith and Uncle Leighton won't let you go to the Convent and you've got to be heathens instead. Father Cassidy – maybe he looks a bit more like Errol Flynn than Gary Cooper, come to think of it – he says it's like God's got this great big book, see, and every time you do something good, it's written down in beautiful gold ink, and every time you commit a sin, it's jotted down in black.'

'A bit like your pay-back book, do you mean?'

'No, I don't! Anyhow, I'm not going to keep that any more, not now I've got a vocation. It's sinful, that pay-back book – I wasn't forgiving those that trespass against me like you're supposed to. With God's pay-back book – I mean ledger – when you get up to Heaven to be judged, they bring it out and tot up all the entries. So I reckon if I make that cake for Aunty Connie as a surprise, it will count as a gold credit. Where's the baking powder kept?'

Cathy thought of her mum trudging all the way up the hill with a heavy basket after shopping in town. Instead of having to turn around and bake the cake when she got home, she could put her feet up instead for a little while. And Isobel certainly seemed full of impressive confidence. She'd stoked the fire and was sieving flour and baking powder into a mixing bowl.

'You need a good hot oven for sponges, so I guess fruit-cake won't be any different,' Isobel said. 'While I'm busy mixing up everything, you can line the baking tin with brown paper. When we get around to the almond icing part, we could even write "Welcome Eleanor Grantby" on the top. Or "Best Wishes to the Two Debs" or something goofy like that. Pity you don't have a nice elegant silver cake stand, though.'

'We've got Mum's old wedding plate with the roses. We always use that for special cakes.'

'It's got a chip out of the side. Just about everything in your house has chips out of it or it's not working or it doesn't match.'

'I shouldn't think saints would worry about things like that,' Cathy said stiffly, and Isobel remembered about her vocation and added, 'Not that I'm saying your house is slummy or anything, even though it is. The rose plate will do fine, we can always bung a doyley on it first to hide the chipped bit, that's if you've got such a thing as a doyley. Now, the eggs . . .'

'Be careful with them, Isobel, they really are the last ones. Freda and Lady Jane stopped laying altogether, and Dot's gone broody and made a secret nest somewhere. We weren't allowed any eggs for breakfast all this week while Mum saved these up for Eleanor Grantby's cake.'

'Any dill can break eggs into a bowl,' Isobel scoffed, and whisked them to a frothy cream, the colour of a morning sunrise. When the mixture was ready, she spooned it carefully into the prepared baking tin and put it in the oven, shutting the iron door. 'There,' she said. 'The important thing with cakes is not to open the door at all for the first twenty minutes, because the draught could make the cake flop. But to be on the safe side, I'll just say a couple of Hail Marys.'

'You seem to be doing an awful lot of praying and that lately.'

'I'm training for the real thing. I said the whole rosary last night kneeling on some haricot beans, asking God to make me holy enough to be a nun. I'd be a lot holier than Sister Eugenie, that's for sure! When I told her I was going to join the order soon as I'm old enough, she reckoned to give her plenty of warning first so she could run off and enlist in the French Foreign Legion.'

'I hope you change your mind, Isobel,' Cathy said, suddenly stricken. 'It means . . . well, we couldn't go to the pictures together any more. And all the other things – making our debut like Grace and Eleanor Grantby and being allowed to wear lipstick and go out at night and maybe allowed to go to the beach all by ourselves . . .'

'Those silly little things don't matter one bit,' Isobel said. 'They're like chaff in the wind or oats or bran or something, I forgot what Father said. Anyhow, once I've taken the veil and I'm inside, I could still wave to you over the Convent fence when you go past. Plus I'll pray like mad you get out of Uncle Leighton's clutches and stop going to that pagan C. of E. Sunday School and be a Catholic instead. And I'll leave you my collection of autographed film-star photos, I already took them down from around my bed and put up a picture of Our Lady instead. I'm aiming to be just like her – you should see all the holy things I've done so far this week! I fetched in the washing without being told and sprinkled all the starched things and rolled them up ready for ironing. And I didn't thieve anything off Mum's dressing-table ever since the Mission started . . .'

'Should we check that cake?' Cathy interrupted fussily.

'I already told you it's fatal to open the oven door even for a peep. It's like when you bake bread – not that my mum ever does. She says it makes her feel too much like a pioneer woman. She doesn't even like reading books about the pioneering women, she says it always makes her feel tired just hearing about all the work they had to do. Has Grace got new gloves and shoes and that for the deb ball? Can I look at them?'

'She always locks her bedroom door when she's at work,' Cathy said. 'She won't even let us in there when she's home.'

'Maybe she left the window unlocked,' Isobel said and they went around the veranda to the front of the house, but the window was sealed tight. 'I could probably force it open with a nail file. There was this gangster film on at the Odeon and a bloke was trapped outside on a skyscraper ledge in a snowstorm, but he found a nail file in his pocket and . . . Maybe I'd better not if I'm planning to be a nun. I guess it wouldn't be very holy to bust into people's rooms. Anyway, Grace might notice the scratch marks on the window sill. I would have liked a gander at her deb clothes, though, seeing you hardly ever get anything new in this house.'

'We manage,' Cathy said defensively. 'It's just Dad hasn't got any money at the moment, it all went into buying that block of land up river. But you wait, we're going to be very rich one day, richer even than Eleanor Grantby. Mum says she's going to take us all into Osborne's and we'll buy complete new outfits starting from pants up . . .'

'Yeah?' said Isobel, not sounding very convinced.

'And if the tung-oil nut plantation doesn't work out for some reason, there's his prospecting,' Cathy said. 'He's got this map another man sold him in a pub. He reckons it belonged to that Lasseter, you know the one who found the gold reef and died before he could show anyone where it was.'

'Good on him,' said Isobel, looking even more unconvinced. 'Hey, something smells funny out on this veranda . . .'

'The cake!' Cathy squealed, and ran back to the kitchen, where dark smoke was pouring busily from the oven door. She grabbed a pot-holder, wrenched open the door and stared at the charred black disc in its tin.

'How did that happen?' said Isobel, amazed. 'After I prayed over it and everything . . .'

'What am I going to tell Mum?' Cathy wailed. 'I'll get killed! Those were the very last eggs and now there'll be no cake for that posh Eleanor Grantby! Fruit-cake's got to be made in advance and stored to bring out the flavour.'

'Aunty Connie can still make one when she gets home. All we've got to do is put things back as they were so she won't even know we had a go at baking. You scrape out the cake tin and tidy up while I go down to the chook-house.'

'But you won't find any eggs – there hasn't been one cackle out of the lazy old things all day! Oh, I'm going to get murdered twice over – first from Mum, then from Grace when she gets home from work! There's only stale gingerbread men in the biscuit tin, and we can't offer those to Eleanor Grantby, even if there's still any left when she comes! Heather made them and she put a little blob of extra pastry on every one on purpose so they turned out rude . . .'

'I'll pray to Saint Anthony. He's supposed to be pretty smart at finding things,' Isobel promised, but when she came back she didn't even have one bantam egg. 'I guess it's because your chook-house is Church of England,' she said. 'I'd offer to run back down to my place, but I know we're right out of eggs. Mum was going to give herself an egg face-mask beauty treatment this morning and there weren't any.

Have we got time to buy some before Aunty Connie gets home? How about that little shop round near the high school?'

'There's no money in the house,' Cathy said in despair. 'With all those new cups and things to buy, Mum was even digging down in the sofa cracks trying to find stray pennies before she went into town.'

'Couldn't you borrow eggs from that nosey lady opposite?'

'No one's home there. She's gone over to East Wilgawa to stay with her daughter.'

'The hospital, then – they should have plenty up at the hospital for the patients' breakfasts. We'll knock on the door of the nurses' home and tell them we're trying to raise money for the Red Cross, only instead of money we have to take eggs to school and sell them for a profit . . .'

'I am *not* going up to that hospital!' Cathy said angrily. 'They think Dad's peculiar always calling in there with inventions he's made. There was this ridiculous lasso thing to stop people swallowing their tongues while they have chloroform, and a bedpan with a rim you fill up with hot water so it's warm to sit on . . .'

'Well then, that only leaves the O'Keefes. They've got plenty of chooks.'

'I can't! We're not allowed to borrow even a cup of sugar off them. They're always down here botting stuff off us, and Mum's getting so fed up with it, she says we're not going to encourage them by doing the same. She'd be really mad if she thought I'd been up to O'Keefes asking for things.'

'She needn't find out. You could take Mrs O'Keefe the eggs back secretly soon as your chooks lay them.'

'Mrs O'Keefe pops in here just about every day and she's a terrible blabbermouth. She's bound to mention it . . . What are you doing, Isobel?'

'Praying for guidance,' Isobel said, flicking little glass beads through her fingers. 'I take my rosary everywhere in my pocket now I've got a vocation. It works, too. Like yesterday, when I was down town real late and had to get the bus home before Mum found out. Only I'd sort of spent the fare already on an ice-cream. But what I did was nip into the phone box and say a quick decade, then got on the bus and told Mr Kelt my mum was at the end of the queue and she was going to pay my fare. There was such a crowd of passengers he never noticed Mum wasn't even there. So don't you worry, Cathy, we'll easily get four eggs before Aunty Connie comes home. Our Lady will help me, seeing I got rid of all those photos of Gary Cooper and Clark Gable and Veronica Lake specially in her honour. She'll tell me what to do.'

'Is she . . . is she coming up with any good ideas?' Cathy asked anxiously.

'You bet she is! Our Lady's telling me loud and clear to go up the back way to the O'Keefes, only not let them spot us,' Isobel said. 'We'll need something to carry the eggs back safely, so bring that funny-looking scone-holder thing your mum made out of Heather's old sports tunic.'

'It's not a funny-looking thing, it's for keeping scones warm at the table when visitors come,' Cathy said, grabbing the scone-holder, which was like a tea-cosy covered with little drawstring pouches. She checked to make sure a new lot of cake ingredients were ready on the kitchen table to replace the ones Isobel had used, and that any tell-tale signs of misguided cooking had been cleared away. Then she followed Isobel across the big paddock and up the track past the sawmill.

'They must all be out,' she said with relief at O'Keefes' fence. 'You always know when they're home, you can hear the din clear down to our paddock. I know where they'll be, out on the river road practising their running. That's about the only thing they ever do. Any time any new kid moves to this town, the first thing the O'Keefes ask is "Are they any good at running?". And if they're not, they go and bash them up first chance they get.'

'Yeah, I know,' Isobel said. 'I remember at school once I saw Danny and Stella O'Keefe chewing lollies in front of a little kid. And he wanted one, so they told him there was a special magic way you could make lollies. They reckoned you had to put a rabbit dropping in your mouth and suck it for ten minutes and it would turn into a lolly, and he believed them!'

'They're disgusting, those O'Keefes. Now we're up here, just what is it we're supposed to do?'

'Our Lady said I should hide out here in the bushes and keep watch while you nip into their fowl-run and look in all the nests. Go on, Cathy, it's all right. It's definitely not stealing or anything, because of all the things the O'Keefes borrow from your mum and never pay back. Our Lady told me.'

'But . . .' said Cathy.

'Don't hang around, they might turn up any minute,' Isobel said, and Cathy tiptoed across the yard towards the fowl-run. She felt she had to tiptoe, even though the house seemed deserted. The grass was stubby under her feet. It didn't get much chance to grow, because when the O'Keefes weren't out on the main road grimly practising running against one another, they held savage pitched battles in the backyard. The grass was as flattened as a field used for heavy artillery.

She opened the little door in the netting fence of the fowl-run and went in. Hens flapped and squawked at her hysterically, but she thought she'd probably be pretty tense, too, if she were a hen belonging to the O'Keefes. She went into the fowl-house and searched the nests, finding one egg almost straightaway, a second in another box further along, and a third, then . . . nothing. She checked all the boxes on the other side, but they were empty. Then, just on the point of giving up in despair, she saw a fat speckly chook watching her balefully from a box up near the roof. She climbed on one of the spattered roosting perches and slipped a hand under the hen's feathers. It darted its head around and gave her a peevish peck on the wrist, but Cathy drew out a warm, freshly laid egg and tucked it into the scone-holder with the others. She went back out into the O'Keefes' yard, latching the fowl-run door guiltily behind her. Now, all she had to do was creep across to the bushes and join Isobel . . .

But Isobel wasn't lurking about in the bushes any more. She was standing by the fence in a circle of O'Keefes, talking with a lot of animation as though her life depended on it. Cathy put the scone-holder behind her back and crept away from them all at a tangent. Maybe Isobel could keep them talking and they wouldn't even notice her ducking away through the sliprail. They certainly couldn't have known about her raid on their fowl-house, or they wouldn't be standing about like that listening to Isobel. She'd be flat on her back under a pile of bodies. Isobel had seen her, then she'd quickly looked away and was chatting with even greater intensity to hold their attention, but as Cathy bent to wriggle through the sliprail, Stella O'Keefe suddenly turned around.

'Oy, Cath Melling, what you think you're doing in our paddock?' she bellowed.

Cathy straightened and stood with her back against one of the upright posts, clutching the eggs behind her. The O'Keefes broke their circle and surged towards her like a mob of wild little brumbies. Isobel came with them, but her face was untroubled.

'Oh, there you are, Cathy,' she said brightly. 'I was just wondering if your mum would change her mind and let you come after me. I was in the middle of telling Stella and them about how I'm going round houses raising money for the Mission. And how you're helping me, even though you've got to go to the rotten old public school instead of the Convent like us.'

'It's not a rotten old public school!' Cathy said and added automatically, 'Public, Public ring the bell, while the Convent march to Hell . . .' only without aggression, because there were rather too many O'Keefes present. They stood in a suspicious bunch about her, staring with shrewd black peppercorn eyes from under their thatchy hair.

'I'm asking each family to give at least five shillings,' Isobel said. 'Five shillings to bring comfort to some poor sufferer in a leper colony. As I was saying to Father Cassidy, I don't mind in the least giving up my spare time traipsing all over town to ask for donations.'

'How come that Father Whatever-he-calls-himself got *you* doing it?' Stella demanded. 'Sister never said anything about it at school. And any rate, they never did anything like that last time they had a parish Mission . . .'

'I volunteered,' Isobel said. 'It's part of my special

devotion to Our Blessed Lady. I'm sure that a measly lousy little five shillings . . .'

'Go shove yer head in a bucket of pig swill,' Danny O'Keefe said rudely.

'Yeah, get lost, Isobel Dion,' Stella said. 'Who's gonna give five shillings to a lot of old lepers? They can't run, even. They haven't got any feet.'

'All right,' said Isobel, looking grieved but full of forgiveness. 'If you won't, you won't, and it's your decision whether you end up in Purgatory for thousands of years or not. But I hope you won't think it's too much trouble to say a prayer for the Mission – in fact I think we should all kneel down right now and go through the whole rosary! Cathy's excused of course, seeing she's a heathen through no fault of her own . . . Oh well, if you don't want to be in a state of grace, and I'd just like to point out to you, Danny O'Keefe, that it's a mortal sin to kick someone holding rosary beads . . . Come on, Cathy, we'll go over to the sawmill and ask the men there.'

Cathy scrambled thankfully through the sliprail.

'Here!' said Stella beadily. 'What's that she got in her hand, that tea-cosy thing . . .'

'That?' said Isobel. 'Oh, I forgot to tell you about that. It's special.'

'It's got lumps in it . . .'

'Little bottles of holy water,' said Isobel. 'They've been specially blessed by His Holiness the Pope. They're on sale for only seven shillings and sixpence and all the money will go to the leper colony.'

'Go jump,' Stella said. 'We haven't got five shillings and we haven't got seven-and-six and you interrupted our running practice. I just beat Dan by three yards . . .'

'You never did, you hairy-legged toad-face boofhead!' Danny yelled. 'Doesn't count if the other one trips up half-way along . . .'

'Does so, too!' the other O'Keefes clamoured and Danny turned on them, cuffing heads and twisting ears.

'You cut that out, Danny, or I'll punch you into the middle of next week!' Stella cried, setting about it, and Cathy and Isobel were able to slip away unnoticed down the track.

As they went in by the back door of the Mellings' house, Mrs Melling was just coming in the front one, laden with all the things Grace had nagged her into buying for Eleanor Grantby's visit.

'How elegant! A dear little guest-towel for the bathroom,' Cathy said, unpacking the parcels from the basket. But first, without Mrs Melling noticing, she transferred the eggs from the scone-holder to the bowl.

'Your bath doesn't even work,' Isobel said snidely. 'You've got to fill it up with water from the copper.'

'Matching cups and saucers and a sugar bowl and . . . ooh, a lovely silver cake stand!'

'I got them all from the second-hand shop for next to nothing, but don't go telling Grace,' Mrs Melling said, taking off her hat. 'Oh, hello, Isobel, love, I didn't know you were dropping in. I met your mother down the street and she was under the impression you're at the dentist, but seeing you're here, stoke the fire up for me and grease the baking tin, there's a good girl. I've got to turn around now and make a wretched fruit-cake, and I'd better not make any mistakes with it, either. Grace is so fussy about having everything just right for her friend's visit. Now, dried fruit, flour, butter, four eggs . . .'

'Here they are, Mum,' Cathy said, handing her the bowl.

'Goodness gracious me!' said Mrs Melling, staring. She put on her reading glasses for a closer look. 'I seem to remember that all those eggs I saved for this cake were white ones, but these are brown! I'm sure they were white – I remember thinking I could maybe save the shells and make nice little Christmas tree ornaments . . . How could eggshells possibly change colour sitting in a bowl?'

Cathy looked quickly at Isobel, but Isobel wasn't troubled.

'I expect it's a miracle, Aunty Con,' she said.

Tyrant

She'd been staying overnight and the arrangement had been that Uncle Tom would drop her off at school when he went to work. But in the morning Aunty Nola said, 'Tom got called away at six, one of the butter factory machines broke down, so you'll have to catch the bus to school, Nance. I've already packed your lunch and you can pick up your nightie and dressing-gown next time you visit.'

'ThankyouverymuchforhavingmeAunty,' Nancy said dutifully at the front door and put up her salt-pale cheek to be kissed, then headed slowly towards the river road corner and the bus-stop. She hated it when things didn't go according to schedule. It made the whole world even more bothersome and alarming than it already was. A big lump of fear, as though she'd swallowed a door knob, blocked her throat as she walked towards the bus-stop. The money Aunt Nola had given her for the fare was slippery with sweat (except Mum always said it was more ladylike to call it perspiration). Oh, she *couldn't* catch that bus, she'd never in her life got on a bus all by herself! Mum was always there, paying the driver, shepherding her to a seat . . .

She stopped just before she got to the corner and peered around a privet hedge. There were crowds of kids waiting at the bus-stop! That loud-mouthed Stewart Thurlow whose big brother had been in a reform school and everyone said Stewart was heading the same way; Cathy and Vivienne Melling who'd walked down the hospital hill; all those terrible O'Keefes who went to the Convent. If it had just been Vivienne Melling on her own, she might have found the courage to go over there and wait for the bus. Vivienne by herself was kind-hearted and friendly, and once at the start of summer, she'd even invited Nancy to her place to play for the afternoon. But now there seemed to be some sort of tremendous battle going on, and the Mellings were involved. One of those O'Keefes had Cathy trapped up in a tree and wouldn't let her down. She was clinging precariously to a branch and he was shaking it for all he was worth, guffawing spit out of his mouth. (Only it was politer to say saliva, Mum said.) Cathy Melling was yelling words that Nancy hadn't ever heard before and trying to kick Danny O'Keefe in the head. Vivienne was clouting him with her school-bag and the other O'Keefes had gathered a pile of dried cow-pats and were hurling them at Vivienne and Cathy. Stewart Thurlow seemed to be just running about throwing punches at everyone in turn.

Nancy stayed out of sight behind the hedge and watched the blue and cream bus trundle along the river road. The driver tooted impatiently and all the O'Keefes and Mellings and Stewart Thurlow stopped what they were doing and swarmed into the bus. Nancy tried to make her feet carry her out from behind the hedge. If she crept onto the bus after everyone else, maybe no one would notice her. Or perhaps only Vivienne, who might call out, 'Hey, Nancy, come and sit next to me!' But what if she didn't? Nancy had no idea of the seating arrangements on the school bus, whether you just plonked yourself anywhere, or if all the seats were allocated beforehand and you had to take the same one each day. And what if Aunty Nola hadn't given her enough money for the fare? Perhaps the driver would think she *had* been given enough money and had deliberately kept aside some to buy lollies (only lollies was common according to Mum, and you should say sweets). Numbed by indecision, she dithered behind the hedge and watched as the bus drew away from the stop and went off down the river road.

Now she'd have to walk all the way to school, and to get there on time she'd have to take a short-cut around by Alma Road (not nasty Greenforest Lane, because Mum had forbidden her to ever walk through there). She set off anxiously down the hill, and her thoughts sped ahead, rushing to meet calamities that hadn't even happened yet.

This was a stock route – what if she ran into a mob of cattle being taken down to the holding yards near the showground? Would there be enough time to climb over into the safety of someone's fenced garden? And if she did, supposing it was someone who had a savage dog? Or – what if she tripped over in all this long grass and knocked herself unconscious on a hidden stone? Bull ants could swarm all over her helpless body and nip her to death! Or a trapdoor spider might bite her!

Whimpering softly with all her worries, she hurried around the corner into Alma Road. It felt so late! There even seemed to be a different, hostile quality about the air, as though it somehow changed from hour to hour. The air around her now was telling her that she shouldn't be here, she should at this very moment be going down the steps into the school quadrangle with a whole safe fifteen minutes before the Assembly bell rang. She'd never been late for school in her life, and if she arrived after Assembly had started, Mr Pratlow would growl at her in front of everyone. She knew she'd die of terror if that happened. She was so scared of Mr Pratlow! Once she'd seen him at the far end of the corridor striding towards her. He'd stopped half-way along to yell through a door at a class making too much noise, and she'd ducked inside a cupboard where brooms were kept. She'd stayed there, quaking, until his footsteps tramped past, even though she hadn't been doing anything wrong in the first place, just running a legitimate message for Mr Smith.

Alma Road and then Slidemaster Street with the corner shop that sold fruit-salad ice-blocks (only Mum wouldn't ever let her buy any because there was no way of checking if the fruit had been washed properly), Curtain Street with its little triangular park and bandstand, Bradtke Street where the Maternity Nursing Home was. (Mum told her that new babies were collected from a special tree in the garden there and given to their mothers.) Every time she passed, Nancy stared over the fence, peering around for a likely tree. She imagined it as covered in downy pink and blue flowers, something like tulips only large enough to hold babies. But now she wasn't so sure. She'd listened to Isobel Dion talking to Vivienne in the park a few weeks ago, and what Isobel said was very peculiar and had nothing to do with tulip trees . . .

Tavistell Street – she couldn't go down there! The Convent was at the other end, and all those kids would chant 'Convent, Convent, ring the bell, while the Public march to

Hell!' over the fence at her. So she went along to the next corner and turned into a street she'd never been in before. She didn't even know its name, but it seemed to lead to Main Street. Oh, golly, she was going to be late and everything was so horrid this morning! Aunty Nola hadn't braided her hair in pretty loops the way Mum did, it just dangled in two straight plaits and one of the bows was coming undone already. She looked as tomboyish as Cathy Melling always did! She scurried along the street with her quivering bottom lip stuck out like a little ledge. A small blue car backed out of a gateway, someone tooted and she got such a fright she tripped over her feet and sat down hard on the pavement.

'Are you all right?' an angry voice demanded, and she nodded speechlessly. 'Then get up at once, you stupid girl! Running along the street like that not even looking where you're going!'

It was Mr Pratlow in the car, glaring at her through his glasses. His little eyes looked like tropical fish in a bowl. 'Nancy Tuckett, 5B,' he barked out of the window. 'You're going to be late for school, Miss!'

'I . . . I . . . I . . .' Nancy whispered.

'Get in,' he said curtly and flung open the door on the other side, and Nancy scuttled into the passenger seat. 'Shut the door, girl!' he snarled and she hurried to obey, not closing it properly the first time and getting yelled at again. He drove down towards Main Street while she sat as still as a book. This was much more scary than the time she'd hidden in the cupboard; it was just as terrifying as though he'd been locked up in that cabinet with her! Every few seconds he snapped out a bad-tempered remark, as though he were firing little bullets at everyone and everything in the Monday morning world of Wilgawa.

'Look at that dog on the road! People should be fined for letting their dogs roam . . . I'll soon find out who owns it and put in a personal complaint! They won't dare let it happen again . . . Get your dusty shoes off those folders on the floor, girl! Haven't you got any common sense – put the folders over on the back seat . . . *No, No, No! Not* like that – hasn't anyone ever taught you not to throw books around? Stack them! Pot-holes – they haven't done a thing about filling in these pot-holes, and I warned them only last . . . Why are those boys skylarking over by the shops when the bell's due to go? I'll have their hides! And who's supposed to be on flag duty? That crossing is to be supervised until everyone's lined up in the quadrangle . . . There's a bicycle left by the fence! Some lazy person is going to be very sorry before the day's done, can't even be bothered going around to the bicycle rack! Get out, Miss, I haven't got all day! Shut the door, were you born in a tent? Off with you and line up . . . Come back here! Haven't you got the manners to say thank you when someone offers you a lift?'

So she wasn't late for school, but some things could be far worse! At Assembly Mr Pratlow said, 'Mr Smith will be absent today due to illness. 5B, listen as your names are called and go to that class-room instead for the day.' To her anguish, she was one of the eight people who were to go to Mr Pratlow's class. She'd always passed that room on tiptoe, pitying the poor 6A girls and boys with all her heart. You couldn't have heard a pin drop in there, because no one would have dared to drop one!

Inside, Mr Pratlow moved people to other desks to make room, then glared at the quaking 5B group as though they were an insect plague. 'Don't think just because your teacher's absent you can slack for the day!' he roared. 'I'll have my eye on the lot of you, don't think otherwise! Now, everyone – clear those cobwebs away!' He took them through all the verses of 'John Peel', marking time with his cane. 5B had no trouble with the tune or the words. He made his own class sing that song every morning before lessons to clear the cobwebs away, and his own voice was so big and powerful it reverberated up and down the corridors and into every room. Only it wasn't like singing, Nancy thought, forming trembling words with her lips even though she was so frightened no sounds came out. It was more like being caught up in a huge cracking, rumbling thunderstorm.

'Mental Arithmetic!' Mr Pratlow yelled. He flung random questions around the room, and if anyone produced an incorrect answer, it was as though he'd caught them with kerosene and matches setting the shelter-shed on fire. Two boys got caned and came back to their desks with agonised palms tucked under armpits but they didn't dare as much as squeak. After Mental Arithmetic, Mr Pratlow wrote two columns of sums on the board, one for his own class and one for the stranded members of 5B, then strode around the room looking over nervous shoulders at exercise books. Occasionally he would smack someone loudly over the head for making an error, and every time he did that the whole class jumped.

Nancy stared, panic-stricken, at the board. She was no good at sums, though nice Mr Smith never minded. Sometimes he'd call her up to the desk and try to explain for the hundredth patient time about fractions, but then he'd look into Nancy's bewildered face and say, 'Oh, never mind, Nance, just do the best you can.' She knew that the best she could do would certainly never satisfy Mr Pratlow. He was nearing the back of the class now and would see that she hadn't worked out even one sum yet! She was almost tempted to peep over at Vivienne's work even though Vivienne wasn't very good at arithmetic, either. But cheating was a sin and Mum said you went to Hell for it when you died. You didn't get carried up to Heaven by the angels and given a dear little pair of feathery wings like Mr Humphreys. Hell was fearsome, ruled by the Devil . . . only she couldn't imagine Satan being quite so frightening as Mr Pratlow with his bully's face and vicious little eyes. He'd finished checking Warren Long's book now, and was heading for the back row – her chin started to wobble with terror – but the morning-play bell rang, sweet as a Christmas chime, saving her.

After recess Mr Pratlow wrote a paragraph on the board for parsing and made 5B attempt it, too. Nancy blinked at her work and gabbled feverishly in her mind, 'An adverb tells how, where, when or why; an adjective is used to describe a noun.' Or was it the other way around altogether? Some people in 6A couldn't remember, either. Mr Pratlow reduced three of them to snivels in a matter of minutes, but he spent so much time bellowing and ranting and snapping sticks of chalk as he jabbed at the blackboard that he didn't manage to get down the back to check Nancy's work.

At lunch-time the sandwiches packed by Aunty Nola could have been filled with wood shavings. Nancy gave them, untasted, to Vivienne Melling whose mother had absent-mindedly wrapped up a tea-cosy and put it in her bag instead of lunch. The playground wasn't even safe, because you couldn't trust Mr Pratlow to stay in his office. He'd charge out tyranically at intervals and stalk the grounds, hoping to catch someone in mischief, and you always knew where he was by the hush that fell over that particular section of the yard, like a big cloud sailing overhead and casting a shadow. She sat miserably on one of the outdoor benches, feeling sick at the thought of a whole afternoon more of Mr Pratlow. No one else noticed what a state she was in, because Nancy Tuckett always did seem to be drooping soggily like a wet mop in some corner not doing anything much for fear of messing up her complicated clothes.

Afternoon was mainly Geography. Mr Pratlow banged his desk so hard that a vase fell off the map cupboard and shattered. A sulky, demoralised silence lay over the tired class-room like smoke, and two more girls were in tears. Nothing could be heard but the scratching of nibs, atlas pages being turned quietly and trapped flies buzzing against the windows. At the end of the day Mr Pratlow kept everyone in for ten minutes because the front row stood up to go before he said they could. Everyone had to sit with hands on tops of heads, perfectly still. When someone sneezed, he added another five minutes.

Mum was waiting for her impatiently at the school gate, but Nancy didn't get the chance to explain that being late wasn't her fault. Mum was too cranky with juggling heavy parcels and in too much of a hurry. 'I wanted you to run a message for me while I take the meat home,' she said accusingly. 'My word, Nancy, what a mess your hair's in!'

'Aunty Nola never . . . I got put in . . . Mr Smith wasn't . . .' Nancy stammered. 'Oh, Mum, I feel poorly! I want to stay home from school tomorrow!' She couldn't, just couldn't face another day in Mr Pratlow's terrible class if Mr Smith wasn't back!

Mum had no sympathy to spare. 'A good dose of castor

oil will have you right by tomorrow,' she said. 'Come along, Nancy, I haven't got any more time to waste. Tweak those creases out of your frock, then you can drop these Mothers' Club lists off at Mrs Whistler's place.'

'But I never . . . I don't even know where she lives. Oh, Mum, I hate going to new places!'

'It's five Tavistell Street, and you won't have to explain anything, Mrs Whistler's expecting them. All you've got to do is wait till she's checked those lists, then bring them straight home. I can't go round there myself, because I've got to get this meat put away out of the heat. Off you go and don't be so silly about it.'

Nancy took the lists, thinking how horrible the whole day was, and getting no better. It was worse than horrible, it was *crook* (even though Mum had forbidden her ever to use that coarse word), because now on top of everything else she had to traipse about in the hot sun doing messages! She trudged away in the opposite direction to Mum, scuffling her new shoes disobediently on the footpath, and because she had her head down nearly ran into Vivienne Melling who was walking along Tavistell Street, too.

'I missed the bus because of that rotten old Pratlow and now I've got to walk all the way home!' Vivienne said. 'What's those papers you've got, Nance?'

'Lists,' Nancy said unhappily. 'For number five Tavistell Street.'

Vivienne swivelled to read what they said, because her eyes were always drawn hungrily to anything with print on it, but these weren't really any more fascinating than their bearer. 'Only Mothers' Club business,' she said, losing interest. 'Your mum's president of that, isn't she? Just as well mine's not – there wouldn't ever be any lists, she'd be scribbling ideas for poems all over them instead! Here's number five, the house you've got to leave them at.'

'Can . . . can you come in with me?' Nancy whispered, mired by bashfulness at the gate.

Vivienne didn't mind, it was an unexpected break in the long walk home, and a bonus came with it, too, because Mrs Whistler had the contents of a jumble sale carton to check before she could sign the lists. She gave them each a glass of cold milk and told them to wait in the back garden until she'd finished. Vivienne helped herself to passionfruit growing over a trellis, to make a passionfruit milkshake, but Nancy sat decorously under a tree and threaded a daisy chain, calming down a little from the stress of the day as she linked each flower. Mrs Whistler's back garden was separated from the one behind by a high paling fence, but one slat was missing. Yawning, she peered idly through and saw a lawn as neat as a starched tablecloth and a lady sitting in a chair on the back porch.

'Ronald!' the lady called piercingly, and Nancy jumped and accidentally made a fingernail eyelet in her own thumb.

'Yes, dear,' someone answered from inside the house.

'These plums have to be picked off the tree before the birds get at them. I told you about that twice already and you still haven't done it!'

'After tea I was going to . . .'

'After tea you've got the car to wash. It's a disgrace, dust and mud all over it, you should feel ashamed, letting it get in that state.'

'Yes, dear, I'll just . . .'

'Haven't you finished putting that washer in the tap yet? Fumbling about, it's quicker to tackle all the jobs myself than expect you to do them properly! Bone lazy . . .

useless . . . never home on time . . . Haven't you made the tea yet?'

'The kettle's just . . .'

'Ronald, I don't want ginger snaps, either, bring me some of those plain digestive biscuits . . . No, they're *not* kept in the biscuit barrel, you fool, they're in that square tin. Like talking to a brick wall . . .'

Poor Ronald, Nancy thought with sympathy, listening through the gap, even though she knew very well that eavesdropping was a sin.

'What an old battle-axe!' Vivienne whispered, coming to look with passionfruit pips all over her chin. 'She's nearly as bad as Mr Pratlow!'

'Ssh!' Nancy whispered back fearfully. 'She might hear you . . .'

But the woman's strident voice whined hatefully on, its owner clearly accustomed to hearing that sound only and nothing else. 'There's a bit of gutter coming loose out here, trust you not to notice it! You never see anything that needs doing around this place – the woodpile's down again, too. I distinctly remember telling you that already this morning, not that you've bothered yourself doing anything about it!'

'She's got a voice like the machinery up at the sawmill!' Vivienne said.

'Ronald – shut the window! The curtain's getting blown about, do you think I've got nothing better to do than wash marks off curtains every day with my poor feet swollen up in the heat?'

'Does she mean she puts the curtains in the copper and treads up and down on them?'

'Oh, shush!' Nancy whispered nervously. 'She might

hear and come and tell us off for listening! She's even *worse* than Mr Pratlow!'

'Ronald, where's that cup of tea? Do I have to wait all week for it!'

The screen door opened slightly and a tray was passed out. The tea maker, blurred by wire mesh, hovered uncertainly, but was neither thanked nor invited to share in the afternoon tea.

'You forgot to put a net cover on the milk jug!' the woman scolded in between sips. 'After you've fixed that washer, you can cut the grass out here – it's all over dandelions. Thought you said you'd do it first thing when you got home? And you left the hose all over the place – you know I like it coiled up . . . A person could trip fetching clothes off the line with their poor swollen feet . . .'

'There, told you so,' Vivienne said, smirking. 'She unpegs the pegs with her toes, too . . .'

'That's another thing . . . that heavy counterpane's been up there on the line since last night getting faded in the sun . . . do you expect *me* to carry it in? *Ronald*, are you listening to me!'

Poor bullied, hen-pecked man, Nancy Tuckett thought with deep sympathy. Poor old Ronald!

Mrs Whistler called out to them that the lists were ready, and Vivienne hastily wiped passionfruit from her face and made sure the extra ones didn't bulge too obviously in her pocket. Nancy worried that no one had thought to tell her stealing was a terrible sin and she'd end up in Hell, but there was something else on her mind, something she wanted to ask Mrs Whistler, just to make sure.

'Who . . .' she said, looking down at the ground.

'Yes, dear?' said Mrs Whistler, not very patiently,

because she was already half closing the door.

'Who . . . lives . . .'

'I'm sorry, dear, you've got such a soft little voice I can't hear you.'

'I think she wants to know who lives in the house behind you,' Vivienne said.

'The Pratlows,' Mrs Whistler said. 'You know Mr Pratlow, he's your headmaster.'

Beach Belles

'You know we're not allowed to go without a grown-up,' Vivienne said.

'Well, I'm practically grown up. I wore Mum's silver high heels down the shops yesterday and never fell over once.'

'Isobel, I'm not going to the beach with you! We'll both get in trouble.'

'What they don't know never hurts them, and anyhow, there's always lots of grown-ups on the bus.'

'They mean we've always got to go with an aunt or a big sister or someone. I don't want to go anywhere, I'd rather stay here and read.'

'Plenty of aunts and big sisters on the beach bus. Doesn't matter if they're someone else's. Oh, come on, Viv! It's on my list of things I want to do before Christmas – go to the beach for the day.'

'Don't you ever give up? We could go to the baths instead.'

'You can't move in the baths on a hot day like this. Everyone flocks there, even Stewart Thurlow. I'm not swimming in water Stewart Thurlow's been in, I might catch foot-and-mouth disease. So if you won't come with me, I'll go all by myself. You can just sit around reading *Pat of Silver Bush*. She's just as much a booby as you are, come to think of it, the way she busts out crying every second page and talks to flowers.'

'We could go to the park . . .'

'If you don't come with me to the beach, I won't play with you all next week! I'll tell everyone at your school you've got worms. I'll rip out the last chapter of *Pat of Silver Bush* so you won't ever find out what happens to her in the end. And – I won't give you anything for Christmas, not even one of those glasses full of popcorn from Woolies!'

'All right,' Vivienne said, defeated. 'But I haven't got a swimsuit.'

'That's okay – I've already packed my old one for you,' Isobel said smugly. 'I knew you'd give in sooner or later.'

The bus for the beach left from outside the post office. Vivienne felt dazed from guilty excitement before they even got on board. She'd never been to the beach before. Every time it was planned in her family, something had happened to prevent it. Grace was going to take them once, but sprained her ankle; and the next time it had rained. Then there'd been the time she came down with measles, striving valiantly to ignore a head that whirled like a merry-go-round. But just as they were all going out the front door, her legs had suddenly folded up underneath her like a new-born calf and Mum saw the rash popping up all over her chest and behind her ears. Heather and Cathy had hated her for days afterwards, and revenged themselves by bringing her a glass of water in bed, and when she'd drunk it they'd told her they'd both spat in it.

'Tell me what the beach looks like,' she kept asking

Isobel, who'd been there plenty of times, because Isobel never let rules and regulations stand in her way.

Isobel was patient at first and said, 'Well, it's kind of big, a lot bigger than the baths. And the water's sort of blue, and there's sand.'

'What else?'

'How do you mean, what else? There's rocks and changing sheds and a little shop where you can buy drinks. And the waves come in and sort of splosh about. It's . . . well, it's just the beach. Stop acting so goggle-eyed and asking so many questions. We don't want people to notice us, do we?'

Vivienne hastily shut up and looked around the bus. There were several people she knew. Mrs Powell was sitting near the front with that uppity Marjorie, but Marjorie pretended not to notice her, so that was all right. There was a crowd of big girls who went to the high school, with two of Heather's friends amongst them, but they didn't deign to notice her, either. There were some of the Sylvesters who lived near the hospital.

'Look at that whacky way Belle Sylvester's got her hair done,' Isobel whispered disparagingly. 'It doesn't even suit her, but she thinks she's just it and a bit now she's left school and training to be a nurse.'

Belle Sylvester, solid, reliable and spectacled, was taking a group of Brownies to the beach. Her face, free of any make-up, glistened with the heat, and all the little Brownies in her care sat as quietly as garden gnomes.

'I was in Brownies once,' Isobel said.

'Were you? You never told me.'

'Only ever went the one time. Mum nagged me into it. Strewth, it was that gruesome! They had these little seats like spotty mushrooms dotted about everywhere. And when they handed in their collection pennies, Belle Sylvester – only they all called her Tawny Owl or Hoot Owl or something – said, "What shall we have today, little Brownies, a big, big pile or a long, long line?" I nearly chucked up! I didn't have a penny to put on the big, big pile, anyway, I'd spent it before I even got there. They shoved me in with the Fairies. They kept hooping their arms up to their shoulders like pretend wings and flitting around the hall every time they had to do anything. So I took off outside while they were all sitting on their mushrooms drinking cordial, only they called it Fairy Nectar. I climbed up on the police station fence and talked to this drunk in the lock-up. So Belle Sylvester called in at my house on the way home and told Mum she didn't think I was responsible enough to be in Brownies yet.'

'Belle's okay. She gave me a dink home on the back of her bike once. And she can't help being plain, Isobel.'

'I just wish she didn't have the same name as me, it's an insult, even though she's shortened it. As a matter of fact, I reckon Belle would suit me more than it does her. When you look at her you just think of a tingy little bell next to someone's sick-bed, but if I shortened mine to Belle, you'd straightaway think of the belle of the ball, stuff like that. You can call me Belle from now on, Vivienne, so I can test it out and see if I like it.'

'All right, Belle,' Vivienne said obligingly.

It was a one-hour trip to the beach and her eyes fastened eagerly upon each new stretch of road. Because she so rarely went anywhere new, everything seemed gilded with enchantment, even a boy sitting by the side of the road eating watermelon.

'"*When I was but thirteen or so*
I went into a golden land,
Chimborazo, Cotopaxi,
Took me by the hand,"'

she recited to herself, remembering a poem Mr Smith had read to them at school.

There was a house with a front garden made entirely of shells; another with an upper storey, like something Pat of Silver Bush might have lived in. She craned her head out of the window as the bus trundled through little hills covered in low bushes and sandy soil. The air became sharp and crisp, filled with an essence . . .

'"*I stood where Popocatapetl*
In the sunlight gleams . . ."'

'Huh?' said Isobel, looking up from her magazine.

'Nothing,' said Vivienne, embarrassed. 'I was just wondering when we'd reach . . .'

The bus suddenly rounded the last bend of the narrow road, turned into a parking space, and there it was, spread out before her – the ocean! So this was the sea – this majestic, restless, rolling thing . . .

'"*I gazed entranced upon his face*
Fairer than any flower –
O shining Popocatepetl
It was thy magic hour . . ."'

She stood in the bus aisle, staring, holding everyone up and quite incapable of moving. Isobel gave her a brisk shove from behind and yanked her down the steps and away. 'Honest, sometimes I think you've got bats in the belfry!' she scolded. 'Standing still and gaping at things like you just saw a holy vision – you're so embarrassing! Come on, first thing we'll do is get into our cossies, then I'll show you how far out I can swim. I'm pretty good, you know, nearly in the same class as Esther Williams. Viv, will you come on! The dressing-sheds are over there.'

Vivienne dropped the lunch-bag, hurrying after her, and had to stop to chase some oranges. She went into a sun-bleached wooden structure, and nearly knocked over two boys who were peeling off their pants. She backed out, scarlet, and found Isobel sniggering in the doorway of an identical building nearby.

'You could have hollered out and told me that was the gents',' she said indignantly.

'Why? It was too good to be true watching you blundering in there! What did you see, anything interesting?'

'Never mind what I saw! I bet you did it on purpose, anyhow. You're a rotten person to have as a cousin sometimes!'

The ladies' dressing-shed was open to the sky and unfloored and smelled of salt. Vivienne balanced on the prickly grass mixed with sand and suffered more humiliation by having to put on Isobel's old bathers, which were far too big and had to be knotted at the shoulder straps to make them stay up.

'You're so small for your age,' Isobel said patronisingly. 'But at least you don't have to worry about your legs being so skinny.'

'Why not?'

'Because they're so skinny no one can see them at all.'

She was wearing her mother's glamorous swimsuit, a two-piece one with a brief bra, and strutted down to the sand, wiggling her hips. Vivienne, who couldn't swim at all, paddled about at the water's edge and watched her gambol far out in green, hump-backed waves, but soon she forgot all about being jealous. There were too many other things to look at: unknown kids who went to the little local school here, the way the foam curled up the yellow sand in a series of loops like copperplate handwriting, then receded as though someone was wiping a slate clean, the great domed sky . . . She was supposed to mind the clothes and towels, as Isobel had ordered her to, but there was a slab of rock jutting into the sea, cratered with little rock pools, as fascinating as a table spread for a birthday party. Vivienne went down on her knees and became part of a telescopic, intriguing world. She found shells as small and delicate as babies' fingernails, and others like tiny, gorgeously coloured turbans. Fish, as bright as earrings, darted through waving forests of bright red blossoms, but when you touched the blossoms, they folded into tight knots. She forgot about being scared of putting her face in water and lay captivated, holding her breath, eyes wide open and grains of sand spangling her eyelashes . . .

'"*The houses, people, traffic seemed*
Thin fading dreams by day,
Chimborazo, Cotopaxi,
They had stolen my soul away . . ."'

'Geeze, if you could only see yourself!' Isobel jeered, thumping her hard on the back. 'Bottom up in the air like someone scrubbing a floor – what is it you're staring at? There's only old shells and starfish in that pool. And you'd better put a towel around your shoulders, because you know what your skin's like.'

'Maybe now I've come to the beach I'll get a suntan like yours,' Vivienne said, but without much hope. Even running about the paddocks she could get sunburnt, and it wasn't fair, because it never turned into a lovely apricot tan like everyone else's sunburn. All she ever had to show for the agony was a fresh veil of freckles.

'No you won't,' Isobel said. 'You'll look like fried bacon unless you're covered, then everyone will know we've been to the beach. Come on out of there now and let's eat. I already spread our lunch things over a table to reserve it.'

'It looks mad, two kids taking up a whole table all to themselves,' Vivienne said uncomfortably when they went over to the picnic area. 'People keep giving us funny looks.'

'So what? We've got as much right as them.' The lunch Isobel had packed wasn't very appetising – meat-paste sandwiches with the edges curling up in the heat, the oranges and stale sliced ginger-roll. 'When I get to Hollywood . . .' Isobel said.

'Hollywood? Cathy reckoned a couple of weeks ago you were on about being a nun . . .'

'That's before I saw the clothes line at the back of the Convent! There's no way I could *ever* spend the rest of my life wearing great big black flannelette bloomers! Anyhow, as I was saying, when I get to Hollywood, I'm going to have a wickerwork picnic basket with plates all different sizes and all matching. And my initials on everything in diamonds, I read in an article once that's what Ginger Rogers has. And a butler to pass everything around . . .'

'Are you kids going to be taking up that table all day?' a cross lady demanded. She was laden with baskets and toddlers. Vivienne started to get up, turning as red as holly berries, but Isobel stayed right where she was.

'My little cousin's just come out of the hospital with polio and it's affected her heart,' she said. 'Her mum said to take real good care of her at the beach. She had to live in an iron lung for months and she gets all out of breath if she has to sit on the ground.'

'Oh, I'm sorry to hear that,' the lady said, and glanced at Vivienne with compassion. 'We'll find somewhere else further along. I hope your health picks up, dear.'

'Isobel!' Vivienne hissed, agonised. 'I've never been in hospital in my life! It's a wonder you don't get a big black spot on your tongue, all the fibs you come out with.'

'I thought I told you to call me Belle from now on.'

'That lady could know someone who knows my mum and what if they say "How's poor Vivienne and her polio?"'

'Stop worrying about things – it drives me nuts. I'm going in for another dip. You better not, because of your polio.'

'But Isobel . . .'

'Belle!'

'Everyone knows you shouldn't swim straight after a meal, you can get cramp and drown. You already went out too far before.'

'That's because I'm not a scaredy-cat like some other people.'

'I am not a scaredy-cat! I always walk over the aqueduct pipes with Heather and Cathy, and no other kids in town are game to do that, not even the O'Keefes!'

'Yes, but the O'Keefes can all swim, can't they? You won't even try and dog-paddle.'

'I thought we came to this beach together! What am I supposed to do while you're way out there showing off in front of all those boys?'

'I happen to be going in for a refreshing swim,' Isobel said tetchily. 'Boys haven't got anything to do with it. You're a pain – I bring you to the beach and all you do is bellyache and accuse people of things they never even had the slightest idea of.'

'I do not! I've been collecting shells for a bangle and looking at things. It's just . . . I thought we could go for a walk along to the cliffs . . .'

'I didn't come here just to look at boring cliffs. I can see them any old time down at the brick works quarry. You can find something to do, make a sand castle . . . Ta ta, see you later!'

Vivienne tidied the remnants of lunch away and went for a solitary, proud walk in the direction of the cliffs. She wasn't enjoying the beach quite so much now. Everything about it was suddenly too large, too overpowering and glittering. Sand clung unpleasantly between her toes and was lodged in her hair, and Isobel – or Belle as she wanted to be called now – was acting so silly out there in the huge waves. She looked ridiculous, anyhow, in her mum's swimsuit, not even properly filling out the top. The way she was skylarking about out there near all those boys – they were all big high-school boys, not interested in someone still at primary school. Vivienne felt forsaken and aggrieved, like a small child sent out of a room during adult conversation.

Leaving the bags and towels to fend for themselves, she walked defiantly along the beach to the cliffs and scrambled over the rocks at their base. There was an opening that led down into a grotto, like a snug little room. Boulders tapered into it, like a flight of steps, so she climbed down easily, jumping the last bit to land on damp sand. The enclosed air was cool there, comforting to skin that was already starting to feel prickly from the sun, and she began to make a castle. Even though Isobel had suggested it in a way meant to be an insult, it was something people in books always did when they went to the beach. Hers was a magnificent castle, decorated with shell fragments and seaweed, and if she'd been feeling friendly towards Isobel, she would have rushed back along the beach and brought her to have a look at it. She scooped out a moat to surround the castle, and a little trickle of sea water helpfully filled it up as she worked.

The sea, kept at bay by the grotto walls, whispered to her; it was like being inside an enormous shell. She constructed a long, winding road leading to a second castle further back inside the cave, and gave that a moat, too. The water followed her inquisitively, and filled the second moat. It nudged gently about her ankles, but a long tendril suddenly snaked past, hissing, then rushed back. She spun around and saw that the front of the little cave was now a green frothy lake and the first castle had vanished completely.

She made a startled dash for the rock staircase, but the remembered easiness of it had somehow altered. Now there was a space before the first step, bridged only by a sheer rock face as tall as she was. She looked at the sea entry, but it belonged now to the water, noisy olive-green water that flung itself about and chattered nastily and gobbled up rocks. While she watched, open-mouthed, the second castle was beseiged and razed.

She couldn't get out – no one even knew she was here and soon the bus would be leaving to go back to Wilgawa! Isobel probably wouldn't even care that she wasn't on it! She'd just shrug her shoulders and get on the bus and open one of her film magazines . . . Vivienne grimly searched the rock face and found a small ledge, just wide enough for a kneecap.

'So this is where you got to!' Isobel said, her head

suddenly blocking out the light above. 'Turn my back on you for one little minute and you sneak off on me without saying! I've been hunting all over the beach for you – I even sent a little kid in the gents' room to see if you'd gone in there again like a dope! That's another thing – you left all our stuff on the sand where it could easily have got pinched if I hadn't spotted it! Come on, Viv, stop mucking around. We have to get changed and catch that first bus home, because the other one doesn't leave till six.'

'Don't you nag at me!' Vivienne snapped. 'I'm coming up as fast as I can.'

'Are you stuck? You'd better not be, the tide's coming in . . .'

'Not really stuck, there's gaps in the wall up to where I climbed down, but I'll have to work them out.'

'You little pest, I'll get into terrible trouble if you drown down there! Everyone will find out we came to the beach by ourselves without a grown-up! And Uncle Leighton won't ever let me go up and play at your house again, not even at Christmas – not that he lets me now officially, but you know what I mean. Come to think of it, you wouldn't be around to play with if you drowned, but there's still Heather and Cathy . . . oh crikey, that water's right up to your knees now – here, try and grab hold of my hand . . .'

'Can't,' said Vivienne. 'If I let go this ledge I'll fall down to the bottom again.' She glanced at her fingers clinging to the slippery rocks, white at the knuckles and the phalanxes flattened with strain. 'I wish you'd just shut up, Isobel, and let me get my breath back.'

'Belle, not Isobel!' Isobel cried. 'Oh, you'll drown, sure as apples! Why did you have to climb down there in the first place? You'll get swept out to sea and bitten in half by sharks! How do you think I'm going to feel at your funeral when I know there's only half of you in the coffin? Careful – you nearly slipped then! Don't budge an inch, just stay right where you are and I'll scoot along the beach and find someone with a ladder . . .'

'No one's likely to bring a ladder to the beach with them,' Vivienne said crossly. 'Anyway, there's no need. If I can just edge further along, there's a bit bulging out and I can . . .'

'Don't even blink!' Isobel wailed. 'You don't know what lives in caves like this – there could be giant octopuses! Any minute a big black tentacle could sneak out from nowhere and curl itself around your waist! I saw that happen in a Tarzan serial at the Roxy . . .'

'Hang on – I'm nearly out . . .' Vivienne said, but when she'd wriggled up far enough to stick her head through the entry hole, she saw that Isobel had run off and grabbed a man fishing from the rocks further along. She was dragging him back by his arm, babbling about blood and sharks and broken legs and a giant octopus. Vivienne scrambled up to meet them, feeling embarrassed.

'You kids playing some stupid game?' the man said angrily. 'Tearing around the beach giving false alarms about people being swept out to sea!'

'Well, she was stuck down in this deep hole . . .' Isobel said.

'I wasn't really,' Vivienne said. 'I told you I could get out.'

'There were huge waves big as engines swooshing right up as far as her neck!'

'They weren't, they were only really up to my ank-'

'I've got a good mind to tell your dad on you. You're

one of the Melling girls, aren't you?' he demanded, looking closely at Vivienne, who went pale under her freckles.

'No, she's not,' Isobel said quickly, tugging Vivienne away. 'Her name's Florentina Bletherby and she's visiting from Sydney while she gets over having polio and we never ever heard of anyone called Melling! Come on, Florentina, we've got to rush or else we'll miss the bus . . .'

'Florentina Bletherby,' Vivienne said when they were changed and sitting in the rear seat behind all the little Brownies with the bus rocking along the sandy road back to Wilgawa. 'No one's called that!'

'Well, you weren't any help, standing there like a stunned mullet. I can tell you one thing – this is the very last time I'm ever taking you along to the beach with me!'

'I never even wanted to go in the first place!'

'Bet you'll blab, too, when you get home. You'll let out that I talked you into going to the beach and your mum will tell mine and I'll cop it.'

'I will not! I never tattle on anyone, Isobel Dion!'

'Belle! I told you a hundred thousand times you've got to call me Belle from now on. I don't like Isobel, it sounds too old maidy. It didn't matter when I had my vocation, because I'd have called myself something nunny like Sister Perpetua or Sister Marie-Madeleine when I took the veil, but now's different. If you don't get in the habit of calling me Belle I won't play with you next week. Plus I'll tell Stewart Thurlow it was *you* who wrote in signing his name and asking for "Christopher Robin is Saying his Prayers" on the request program!'

When the bus got back to Wilgawa post office, Vivienne's skin felt seared and tender. She would have liked to go to Isobel's house and dab it with cold tea, but Isobel was sick of her company now and didn't invite her. She just snatched up the bag holding the wet towels and swimsuits and said bossily, 'Just you remember – we spent all afternoon in the orchard knitting rug squares to raise money for the Red Cross.'

Vivienne plodded up the river road, her shoulders stinging where her dress made contact. When she reached home, she strolled in with an air of virtue, like someone who'd been knitting rug squares all afternoon, but Cathy looked at her pink, sand-streaked face and said accusingly, 'You've been to the beach!'

'No I haven't!' Vivienne said, but the little paper bag clutched in her hand suddenly split under its damp weight, and turban-shaped shells rattled all over the floor.

'Mum! Guess where that Vivienne's been – she's been sneaking off to the beach!' Cathy cried, mad with jealousy, and Mrs Melling looked up from her typewriter.

'You know very well you're not allowed to go to the beach unless there's a grown-up along!' Mum said sternly. 'Just what have you got to say for yourself, Miss?'

'I went with . . . with Belle,' Vivienne said sulkily. 'She asked me to.' She didn't see why she should cop all the trouble, and trouble there undoubtedly would be, because Mum had her jaded, fed-up-with-everything face on and likely to jump hard on any child who annoyed her this evening.

'Belle Sylvester?' Mum asked, and after a second or two Vivienne nodded. Belle Sylvester, after all, had been on the bus, so they'd certainly shared the trip. 'Well, I suppose that's all right, then,' Mum said. 'She's such a nice sensible girl, doing nursing up at the hospital and running Brownies. It was very kind of her to take you, and I hope you remembered to thank her properly.'

But Vivienne was down on her hands and knees retrieving all the little shells. She'd make a beautiful Chimborazo, Cotopaxi bracelet after tea, and never let Cathy wear it.

Lady Muck

Grace walked apart, looking down upon everyone and everything in Wilgawa. At meal times she delivered lectures upon being uncouth. Treacle tart was uncouth, so were elbows on the table and butter slathered straight onto bread instead of being placed daintily at the side of a bread-and-butter plate.

'Eh? What's a bread-and-butter plate?' Cathy asked, and Grace, frowning, said that Cathy was the uncouthest thing of all.

Occasionally they had to run up to the public telephone outside the hospital with a message for Grace at work. 'Good morning,' she'd say in a plummy voice copied from British films. 'Robinson's Furniture Emporium . . . this is Grace Melling speaking, may ay assist you?'

'Knock it off, Grace! Listen, Mum says after work you gotta pick up some chook feed at the Hay and Corn Store . . .'

'Oh, it's only *you*!' Grace would hiss over the phone in her normal voice. 'Don't you *dare* ring me at work! And I'm certainly not being seen going into anything so uncouth as the Hay and Corn Store!'

When she came home from work she unwrapped a parcel that certainly wasn't chook food. 'Don't any of you *dare* put your filthy little paws anywhere near it!' she said fiercely. Because she was so tall and superior and alarming, Heather, Cathy and Vivienne stood back from the dining-room table and obediently put their hands out of sight. Grace scrubbed the table with sandsoap, then covered it with clean paper before she spread out the length of white material.

'Oooh – it's all shimmery like a cloud!' said Vivienne. 'It's beautiful!'

'If you ask me, it looks like something they'd wrap up a dead body in,' Heather scoffed.

'No one *is* asking you,' Grace said witheringly. She pinned pattern pieces carefully to the material and opened the scissors.

'Barbara Sylvester's sister's having watered taffeta,' Cathy purred. 'It's got little ripples over it like waves – *and* she bought it ready-made from Osborne's, not just run up on a sewing-machine.'

'Doreen Sylvester is going to look exactly like a big fat round of cheese, and you don't know anything about dress designing, so shut up,' Grace said. 'Let's see . . . I wonder if I'll have enough material to make a Grecian drape at the shoulder . . .'

'You could always *urn* some more,' said Heather.

'Do ruffles round the hem!' Vivienne begged. 'And a sweetheart neckline and puffed sleeves . . .'

'I've got a much better idea,' Cathy said. 'She should just make a big white sack that fits over her head so no one can even see her.'

'*Mum*!' Grace called angrily. 'Can't you keep these

detestable uncouth children out from underfoot?'

Mum set them all to work filling a new mattress cover with kapok, a job which they loathed. 'Leave your sister alone while she's making her dress,' she said severely. 'This is the first deb ball we've had since the war ended, and it very nearly didn't happen with the Mechanics Hall getting flooded last winter. So even if it is on at the wrong time of year so close to Christmas, it's still a big occasion in Grace's life and I won't have her upset.'

'It's a wonder she even got someone to partner her,' Heather muttered, holding open the end of the mattress cover while Vivienne and Cathy filled it with nose-tickling kapok. 'Who'd want to dance with *her*? She'll be pinching them every time they make a mistake and standing with her nose up in the air not speaking to them during the supper. She's awful! Isobel's mum gave her those bonzer silver sandals and she wasn't a bit grateful, just went down to Bailey's and swapped them for those ugly plain white things.'

'And she won't even let us see her new petticoat with the lace, just like she won't let us watch her cut out that dress,' said Cathy. 'I'm sick of Lady Muck and her old deb ball!'

But it dominated the whole house for days. No one was allowed to use the dining-room table in the evenings while the precious dress was being assembled, and when it was finished, Grace tried it on secretly in her room and still wouldn't let them see it. She put it away in her wardrobe with the new shoes, a fine lawn hanky trimmed with gossamer lace and a little evening-bag embroidered with silver bugle beads. Right up to the time of the ball she didn't have to help with the washing-up or any of the housework, because she was trying to keep her hands nice.

'It's not fair!' wailed Heather, Cathy and Vivienne, but this was the first debutante Mum had ever had in the family, and she was making the most of it.

'You children can just stop being so selfish! You know very well Eleanor Grantby's staying overnight to make her debut with Grace – I thought I told you to help by cleaning out that pot-cupboard yesterday! Not one of you has even lifted a finger . . .'

'Eleanor Grantby's not likely to look inside the pot-cupboard,' Heather said. 'And you don't even notice what the house looks like most of the time. It's only when we get visitors you put on a big . . .'

'I beg your pardon, Miss!' Mum said ominously and Heather hastily changed her tune.

'. . . it's only when we get visitors you put on an apron and wear your fingers to the bone with a lot of extra work.'

But Mum was distracted by something she'd just noticed on the veranda ceiling. 'Who scribbled that rude limerick about Grace!' she cried. 'You can just stop accusing each other and Isobel when she's not even here to defend herself. What would Eleanor Grantby think if she read something like that! One of you climb up on a chair this instant and rub it off! The whole veranda's got to be washed, too, and I don't mean just a lick and a promise with a damp mop, either. All those cobwebs have to come down – Cathy, get the broom and see to it.'

Isobel turned up while they were slaving away on the veranda. 'Is your dad . . .' she began.

'No, he's not,' Heather said crossly, on her knees beside a dish of soapy water. 'Grace made sure of that. She doesn't want him around embarrassing her when Eleanor Grantby's here, so she told him a farmer found a lot of gold dust in the river way up near Baroongal Flats. Dad's gone haring off there to set up camp and prospect. And if you didn't annoy him so much when he's home, Isobel, he wouldn't have such a spite against you. Every time Mum talks him into giving you another chance, you go and do something else to upset him.'

One time she'd been there, Isobel had taken one of his most prized possessions, the Turk's fez he'd brought back from fighting in the first World War. She'd worn it down to the shops, with the tassel dangling at a rakish angle, but he'd been unexpectedly in town that day and spotted her. Isobel claimed he'd chased after her, roaring like a buffalo, all the way up Main Street and she'd had to nick into the corset department of Osborne's and take refuge in the fitting room.

She watched the preparations for Eleanor Grantby's visit, but didn't offer to help. 'I only really came up to see Grace's deb dress,' she said. 'I know it won't be much seeing you're so poor, but I've already had a look at everyone else's in town. Doreen Sylvester and that big blimpy Sheila Hawke who lives over on Alma Road and the Edwards girl . . .'

'How?' Heather asked. 'You don't even know the Edwards or the Hawkes.'

'Oh, I got in,' Isobel said carelessly. 'It was easy. I just knocked on their doors and tried to look younger than I am and put on a silly babyish voice and asked their mums if I could see the pretty deb dresses. You should have heard me! I sounded just like Viv at her soppiest! They liked having someone to skite to. The other mums don't hand out any praise because they're all so jealous of other girls maybe showing their own one up. No danger of that with Grace, though. She's no competition to anyone. She'll just look like a maypole wrapped up in white. You should see Margaret Edwards' dress – it's white net with a crinoline! And Sheila Hawke's is all tiny little frills sewn in layers like a pineapple!'

'Lady Muck won't even let us see hers till tonight,' Cathy said. 'She couldn't even care less if she makes her debut or not. She says it's a bit uncouth unless you can do it properly and be presented to the King and Queen at Buckingham Palace. I guess the Wilgawa Mechanics Hall and the Mayor and his wife aren't really the same thing when you think about it.'

'Who's Lady Muck's partner?'

'Anthony Robinson – you know, his dad owns the shop where she works and he's got big stick-out ears like wheat harvesters,' Cathy said. 'Grace despises him, but she doesn't like any of the other boys in Wilgawa, either. Oh, she's such a snob! She didn't really want him to come out here and pick her up tonight so he'll find out she lives in Sawmill Road, but Mum won't let her get a taxi down to the hall and meet him there instead. So they're all going down together in Anthony Robinson's dad's car – Grace and Anthony and Eleanor and her partner and Mum crammed in like sardines. Grace says soon as we hear that car out the front we all have to stay out of sight under the dining-room table or she'll hit us.'

'Can't I have a look at her dress now? I mean, I know it's not even going to be worth looking at, but I came up all this way when I could have been down at the Roxy watching *Goodbye Mr Chips* even though I can't stand that Greer Garson. She talks as though she's got a mouthful of tacks – just like Grace, come to think of it.'

'Well, maybe if you're quick. She's down the back

drying her hair in the sun, and there's a chance she's left her bedroom door open . . .'

For once, Grace had, and Isobel raced across to the wardrobe and took out the deb dress on its crocheted hanger.

'Grace designed it all by herself and drafted the pattern and everything,' Vivienne said proudly.

'She's wearing . . . this? She's going to be a proper laughing stock if she goes to the deb ball dressed in this!' said Isobel, and Vivienne stopped feeling proud. She inspected the dress uncertainly. It was very plain, with a simple round neckline and bell-shaped sleeves, and there wasn't one bow or frill or ruffle anywhere.

'Serve her right if everyone *does* laugh at her!' said Heather with satisfaction. 'Nasty conceited thing she is! Hey, did you know there's a chance she might be going to the city after Christmas? Our Aunty Elsie offered to pay the fees for a dressmaking course and let her board there, so Grace sent away for the entry form . . .'

'Pity she couldn't have gone there before she started on this dress! Margaret Edwards has oodles of material in her skirt, her mum said it took a whole night just doing the gathering. And Sheila Hawke's got appliqué lace butterflies sewn all over her bodice.'

'Maybe . . . maybe it will look different when Grace puts it on,' Vivienne said.

'Worse, you mean! Margaret Edwards had a perm done specially, but I bet Grace hasn't even put her hair up in pin curls. Your sister's going to shame you. They always take a group photo of those debs, you know, and hang it up in the *Gazette* window. Everyone in town goes to look at it specially. Geeze, I feel that sorry for you kids with everyone knowing Grace is your sister! Still, maybe they'll stick her on the end of the line for the photo and make sure it gets cut off at that point so she won't show up. It would be more tactful, really.'

'Good!' said Heather. 'It'll just put her nose right out of joint not being in that photo, no matter how much she pretends not to care!'

'What are you brats doing in my room?' Grace said at the door, imperious and terrible, and Heather quickly closed the wardrobe with the dress safely inside.

'There was this whopping great big blowfly,' Isobel said. 'We chased it all through the house trying to get it outside, only it flew in here. It's okay, though, Viv just flapped it out the window. We knew you wouldn't want it buzzing around in here when your friend comes.'

'Nor do I want grubby little uncouth girls,' Grace said loftily. 'Weren't you all supposed to be cleaning the veranda? I want it absolutely spotless before Eleanor comes and I'll be out to check in exactly ten minutes! Isobel, you can run along home now, seeing I've got company coming.'

'Oh, I don't mind helping them tidy up,' Isobel said, and they looked at her, amazed, but out on the veranda she added, 'It's really only because I want to stay and have a squizz at Eleanor Grantby's dress. Don't let me hold you up or feel that you've got to entertain me or anything – I'll just sit here on the steps and read this article about the mansions of the Stars.'

Eleanor Grantby arrived at four-thirty, travelling down on the mail van. They all hung about while she unpacked her suitcase, feeling relatively safe because Grace was putting on an indulgent, caring big-sister act for her benefit, and couldn't order them out. She glared ferociously at them behind Eleanor's back, however, and jerked her head meaningfully towards the door, but they pretended not to see.

'Oh, now that's what I call a deb dress!' Isobel cried as Eleanor unfolded it and put it on a hanger.

'Grandma sent away for it to Sydney,' Eleanor said rather smugly. 'I was going to make one, like Grace did, but Grandma said it was such a special occasion and we could lash out a bit. Oooh, I am looking forward to tonight, aren't you, Gracie?'

Grace nodded and smiled sweetly, but behind Eleanor's back she was prising Cathy's inquisitive hands off a box of talc with enough force to crack the bones.

'How do you like the new blind on Grace's window?' Vivienne asked sociably, enjoying the novelty of having a visitor to stay. She preferred to forget Rita's visit in November because it had been such a disaster.

'It's very nice,' Eleanor said. 'Unusual, having stripes like that, but Grace always was so artistic. Oh, Grace, won't it be lovely if you can get into that dressmaking course . . .'

'Dad found this bit of canvas down on the tip,' Cathy said, sucking bruised knuckles and getting her own back. 'He brought it home and Mum scrubbed all the mildew off and Grace cut it out and . . .'

'Eleanor, you'd probably like to eat early after your trip,' Grace interrupted. 'I'm afraid it's nothing much, just a light meal. These children will be having their tea later on, after we've gone.'

Before Eleanor's arrival she'd set the table daintily with fragile crustless sandwiches, tiny egg-and-bacon pies, lemon-curd tarts and the beautiful iced fruit-cake as a centre-piece. Isobel, Heather, Cathy and Vivienne knew from the blood-curdling glances she shot at them, that they weren't to touch as much as a slice of cucumber. Eleanor, who seemed to have a very healthy, wholesome appetite, ate most of it, anyhow, and listened to Grace chatting in a high-flown manner in her poshest voice.

'That's may father's collection of war relics,' Grace said, pointing to the rusty bayonets and swords hanging above the sideboard. 'They're quaite valuable. He's very interested in military history . . .'

'He said the best bloody time he ever had in his whole life was fighting in the desert,' Cathy volunteered. 'He reckons it beat bloody farming any day. He tried to get into this last war, too, so he could do some more fighting, but they said he was too bloody old . . .'

'Cathy!' Mum and Grace both said together.

'What's the matter?' Cathy said, aggrieved. 'I'm only telling it exactly how Dad does.'

'Where is your dad, Grace? Isn't he coming to the hall tonight to see you make your debut?' Eleanor asked. 'My father was really sorry he couldn't leave the farm.'

'Dad's away – unfortunately,' Grace said. 'He had to travel up river on urgent business and I'm very, very disappointed he couldn't be home to see me in my deb dress.' She slapped Vivienne's hand viciously away from a lemon-curd tart. 'Certain other people may not be allowed to see me in my new dress, either, if they don't stop making barbaric little pests of themselves . . .'

'Yes, you're to stay right out of the way while Eleanor and Grace and I get ready,' Mum said. 'There's to be no running in and out. You'll be able to see what the girls look like when they're all dressed, and not a moment before. Oh . . . I didn't realise you were here, too, Isobel. It's getting late, won't your mum be expecting you home?'

'Well, it's kind of dark now, Aunty Connie,' Isobel said. 'She wouldn't want me to be walking home in the dark, specially on an empty stomach. I know – I could get a lift back when you go down to the ball. You could just drop me off at my place . . .'

'We certainly can not!' said Grace. 'I'm not asking Anthony Robinson to drive out of his way, and there won't be any room in the car, either.'

'Oh well,' Isobel said. 'I'd better be off then – down past that creepy old cemetery, past all those tramps who hang around in there drinking plonk. Not to mention Greenforest Lane. But never mind, I expect I'll be all right. I could borrow one of Uncle Leighton's old swords for protection . . .'

'Oh dear,' Mum said worriedly. 'No, it really is too late for the child to be wandering about the streets, and she'd better sleep here on the sofa. We'll just have to ask Anthony to make a detour, Grace, so I can let Isobel's mother know where she is.'

'Little pest!' Grace said furiously.

'There's no need to call in and tell my mum,' Isobel said, knowing that she certainly wouldn't be sleeping on the lumpy old sofa – she'd make Vivienne sleep there and take her bed instead. 'I already told her before I came up here I'd be staying overnight.'

'Well, just as long as you all keep out of the road while we get dressed,' Mum said. 'But I'll need someone to lace me into my corset first.'

After they'd done that, they went and sat on the veranda, swatting at mosquitoes in the dusk and feeling like Cinderella.

'That Grace is so mean!' Cathy said. 'She had a whole

lot of scrap material left over from the dress, but she wouldn't even give me any to make hair ribbons. Not letting us in to watch them get dressed is the last straw! I'm keeping my fingers crossed she ladders her stockings!'

'I'm hoping she gets a big scorch mark on her dress like that girl in *Little Women*,' said Heather.

'Well, she's going to look a fright, anyhow,' Isobel said. 'She won't let me do her front hair with the curling tongs, so she'll be going off to that deb ball looking exactly like she always does . . .'

'A prune-faced, prissy-looking bean pole!' Heather jeered. 'I wouldn't be surprised if Anthony Robinson takes one look and drives straight off back down the hospital hill without her!'

'You can't help feeling a bit sorry for her, though,' Isobel said. 'I mean – having to watch Eleanor Grantby get all dolled up in that expensive frock, and Eleanor's kind of pretty, too, with those big brown eyes like a Jersey cow . . . Poor old Lady Muck, she's going to look like something the cat dragged in.'

'I hope she doesn't,' Vivienne said slowly. 'I mean . . . I think she's bossy, too, but I want her to look a bit nice for the deb ball – just as nice as anyone else's sister.'

Darkness blotted out the paddock, and the grazing cow became invisible, just a nearby disembodied sound of tail-swishing and a contented munching of grass. Lights appeared in all the hospital windows up on the hill and the mosquitoes came out in great whirring clouds, finally driving them inside where they weren't particularly wanted. Mum was dashing about in her good floral rayon and her paste necklace, desperately hunting for a needle and thread to sew on a snapped suspender. She glanced at the mantel clock, gave up the search and used a shilling to twist her stocking top through the suspender and anchor it that way.

'You look really nice!' Vivienne said, thinking how Mum rarely had the chance to dress up and go anywhere special.

Mum went pink with pleasure and stood for a minute looking at herself in the mirror, something else which she hardly ever did. 'When I was Grace's age I used to have such pretty hair,' she said. 'Coppery, like yours and Cathy's. It came all the way down to my waist when I brushed it loose . . . My goodness, what am I doing, wasting time like this! There's a scuff mark on one of Grace's new white shoes . . .' She rubbed at it frantically with a slice of bread, ordering them, when they offered to help, to sit out of the way in a row on the sofa and not budge.

'Mrs Melling!' Eleanor called. 'Oh, please . . . can you come and fix this earring? The screw's come right off . . .'

'I wish now I'd called in and watched Doreen Sylvester get dressed for the ball instead,' Isobel said. 'Or stayed home and got my Dorothy Lamour scrapbook up to date. I mean, it would be worth it if we were going to see something terrific at the end of all this waiting about, but we won't! Eleanor will look okay, but it's going to be embarrassing, really, thinking up something nice to say to Grace.'

'Tell her the truth – that she looks like something the cat dragged in,' Heather said. 'It won't matter, bossy hag that she is. Anyhow, soon as they leave, we can polish off the left-over sandwiches and cake. And Viv can fry up some chips and we'll make Gutsy Drinks . . .'

'And try on Eleanor Grantby's dressing-gown and nightie,' Cathy whispered, because the door of Grace's room was finally opened and Eleanor came mincing out on a cloud of Evening in Paris perfume.

'Doesn't she look a picture?' Mum said, beaming.

'She looks grouse!' said Isobel. 'Just like a film star, no kidding!'

Eleanor, smirking as though she personally held the same opinion, waltzed up and down the hallway for their benefit, holding up the long skirt of her ruffled dress. Her petticoat was ruffled, too, and the satin sash of her dress tied in a big bow at the back. There were more bows on her sleeves and she wore a spray of pearl flowers in her wavy hair. She looked, Vivienne thought dubiously, like one of those plump Kewpie dolls on sticks you could buy at the Show; all she lacked was a sprinkling of silver glitter . . . But the others were crowding around her full of admiration, making her show off her curtsy and begging to be allowed to hold her bouquet in its lace holder.

'I think I can hear a car out the front!' Mum said excitedly. 'Oh dear, I hope they don't get stuck in that silly trench Dad started digging when we thought the country was going to be invaded and he was going to make us all get in there and defend it to the death . . . Come along, Grace, you mustn't keep the boys waiting . . .'

Grace came out, not particularly hurrying herself, and they turned from Eleanor and looked at her. She'd braided her long hair on top of her head like a crown and fastened it with a single white rose. Not even glancing in the sideboard mirror, she smoothed on her white gloves, picked up her small posy and opened the front door.

'There!' Isobel whispered triumphantly to the others. 'I told you, didn't I? It's so . . . plain!'

It is plain, Heather thought. But . . . she sort of looks like one of those tall elegant lilies . . .

'Geeze, I feel sorry for poor Aunty Connie having to sit with all the other mums and they'll know that's her daughter!' Isobel said.

Grace kind of makes Eleanor Grantby look like a big frilly simpering baby! Cathy thought, surprised. It's like . . . when she gets to the ball, she shouldn't have to curtsy to anyone, they all should be curtsying to *her*!

They stood in the doorway and watched Grace and Eleanor and Mum go out to the car. While the others squeezed themselves in, sorting out trailing hems and bunched-up petticoats, Grace stood aloofly apart in the moonlight.

Oh, she looks just like the Lady of Shalott! Vivienne thought, her heart giving a sudden aching lurch. She looks like a goddess! Our Grace is going to make all those other girls at the ball want to curl up and die! She's the couthest thing in all of Wilgawa, and she isn't just pretty – she's . . . beautiful!

'Well, didn't I tell you so?' Isobel said as the car and its passengers whisked up the hill towards the hospital and out of sight. 'Didn't I say all along she'd look like something the cat dragged in!'

But to her utter astonishment, Heather and Cathy and Vivienne swung around indignantly and hit her.

Deck the Hall with Boughs of Holly

'That's uncouth!' Grace said, frowning at the brooch, which was shaped like a gold boomerang with letters running across it spelling out 'Mother'. 'It's so hideous Mum would probably think it's elegant, seeing she's got about as much taste as you have. Put it back. You'd better hurry up and find something else, because we've got to meet her at four and help carry home the groceries.'

'I can't find anything for two shillings,' Vivienne said in despair. She thought that maybe she'd have to go to Woolworths after all, and settle for buying hankies, though hankies always looked so stingy as presents, no matter how well you wrapped them in fancy paper with Christmas seals and tinsel . . .

'Hurry up! Dragging me in here with you – I don't want people to know our family buys Christmas presents from the second-hand shop!'

'Not only Christmas presents. I wanted you to come with me because you're really good at picking out old things no one else would even look at twice. Remember that velvet cushion cover you sewed up into a bolero . . .'

'Will you keep your blabby voice down! I don't want everyone in Wilgawa knowing I wear a cushion cover, specially one that came from Valdoone's! Make up your mind quickly, Vivienne, and let's get out of here. What about that little Toby jug?'

Vivienne went back to her indecisive hovering over the bric-à-brac, rejecting the Toby jug because its red face reminded her of Mr Pratlow. There were necklaces, but all quite ordinary, plain black beads or long strings of amber. A fan – there was a nice one with only one spoke missing at the back of the shelf – but Mum already had an ivory fan, a memento of her girlhood, carefully wrapped in tissue paper in the chest of drawers.

'It's so hot in here,' Grace complained crossly. 'The sun on that iron roof makes it like an oven and there's always a funny smell. I absolutely loathe and detest the smell of second-hand furniture and old books and lino. Oh, I can hardly wait to get away from Wilgawa and board with Aunt Elsie in the city! I still can't believe she's invited me and she's going to pay for the course and everything – just think, studying drafting and dressmaking and the chance of getting a decent job once I'm through! I'll only ever buy brand new things for the rest of my life and never go into a second-hand shop ever again! Only three more weeks, I'm just counting the days till . . .'

'Don't!' Vivienne whispered, and Grace looked at her in surprise.

'It's just . . . it's going to be . . . peculiar when you go,' Vivienne said awkwardly. 'Old Mrs Farrer's always talking about things like that. She's got five children and she's always telling me over her fence about how they all grew up and moved away. She said . . . oh, it was *sad* . . .'

'What was sad?'

'She said for a while after each one left, she still kept setting their place at the table by mistake. I reckon that's exactly what Mum will be doing when *you* leave after Christmas, you know how vague she is. A place set for a person at a table – only they won't be coming in through the door like they usually do ever again . . .'

'Don't be so soppy, Vivienne. It's only natural – families grow up and people get married or move away to the city so they can get better jobs. You can't expect things to stay the same for ever,' Grace said crisply, but after a moment she added with more gentleness, 'How about that little china shepherdess for Mum? It's sentimental, but she likes corny things.'

'I don't want to buy that – all the gold's come off the bonnet. There must be something else, something nicer . . . Oh, Grace – look!'

'Will you please stop yelling and embarrassing me in public places! Now what's the matter?'

'Look! There's a plate here exactly the same as Mum's rose plate she got for her wedding! It's chipped, but Mum's one at home has a chip out of it, too, so it wouldn't matter! If I bought this she'd have one nice plate for cake when visitors come and another matching one for scones. Oh, fancy finding it just like that – the exact same pattern!'

'It hasn't got a price tag on it. How do you know you'll have enough money?' Grace said, but Vivienne was already scooting between the ancient cots and armchairs, dusty old pianos and wicker commodes to ask Mrs Valdoone at the counter how much it cost.

'Twelve shillings. That's very high-quality fine bone china.'

'Twelve shillings! But . . . but it's got a chip out of the rim!'

'Not so you'd notice. Those roses are hand-painted, too, you can see all the little brush strokes. Some people collect nice old plates like that, and I can't just let it go for a song.'

'I want to buy it for someone for Christmas,' Vivienne pleaded. 'Someone who'd really love it! If I put two shillings down – that's all I have – would you let me take it now and pay what I can afford each week till it's all paid off?'

'Vivienne!' Grace hissed at her, scandalised, and Vivienne remembered Mum's firm rule: if you can't afford to pay cash, then you don't really need it, and want must be your master. Only – in some cases that couldn't possibly apply! She couldn't afford this perfect, ideal gift, and it wasn't really needed, but if she had to walk out of the shop and risk someone else buying it, she'd . . . die!

'You can lay-by it, but I certainly couldn't let you take it off the premises until it's fully paid for,' Mrs Valdoone said disobligingly, not swayed in the least by Vivienne's urgent face. 'Anyhow, there's plenty of other things to choose from if you've only got two shillings. That china shepherdess, for instance, that's a real bargain. Or there's this sewing-case, the hinges are a bit rusty, but nothing a little bit of elbow grease wouldn't fix.'

Vivienne scowled at the ugly sewing-box and turned blindly towards the door, but Grace tugged her back. 'I've got seven shillings,' she said. 'If we put our money in together, perhaps we could . . .'

'That still only makes nine,' Mrs Valdoone pointed out. 'I've got no intention of just giving things away . . .'

But Mr Valdoone, so gentle and shadowy that

customers tended to forget he was there, unexpectedly glanced up from the accounts ledger and cleared his throat. 'Oh, go on with you, El, let the young ladies buy the plate if they want it that much,' he said. 'Christmas present for their mum, I'd imagine.'

'Nine shillings for an old plate, not to mention having to stand there and get glared at while that dragon Mrs Valdoone was wrapping it up!' Grace scolded when they were out in the alleyway. 'She didn't like poor little Mr V. shoving his nose in like that, you could tell, and I bet he's getting told off for it now. Oh, I must have been mad – I was planning to get Mum lisle stockings from Osborne's. You and your silly impulses!'

'Mum will like this a whole lot better than stockings,' Vivienne said, tenderly clutching the parcel done up with brown paper and twine. 'Only you're not to write "From Grace" in big letters on the tag so there's hardly any room for me. Oh, that's another thing, I haven't got any money for wrapping paper – can I have some of yours? I only need a little bit. Pencils is what I bought for everyone else.'

'A pencil?' Grace said. 'Is that all I'm getting from you for Christmas?'

'It was going to be a surprise,' Vivienne said, crestfallen. 'Yours is a nice one, though. It's striped, with a tassel and a rubber on the end. You can use it to write letters home when you're . . .'

But she didn't want to think about Grace leaving home next month. Such thoughts didn't fit in with the preparations for Christmas, didn't belong to the summery day and the excitement of Main Street filled with people from out of town doing their last-minute shopping. There were jolting reminders, however, at every corner as they went along to meet Mum and help carry the groceries home. Grace was stopped constantly by people who'd heard that she was going to the city to learn dressmaking. She stood, trapped on the footpath by kindly people who'd known her all her life, but Vivienne didn't want to listen to utterings like, 'We all hope you'll be coming back, Gracie, after you finish your course. It's sad when the young ones leave Wilgawa . . . I hope it's not for good, love. Your mum and dad will miss you . . .' Grace murmured polite things, but Vivienne closed her ears and concentrated instead on Bailey's shop window.

She laid her palms flat on the window and gazed with an intensity almost powerful enough to shatter the glass, at something she'd been covetting ever since Bailey's put their summer stock on display. The patent shoes were decorated with a flat grosgrain ribbon bow and the toe-caps had a perforated pattern of tiny spearheads, though Isobel, who knew everything, had said they were called 'fleurs-de-lis'. Isobel had also said she wouldn't be seen dead in kiddy shoes like those, and was saving up for a pair of bottle-green suede high-heels. But to Vivienne they were the most wonderful shoes she'd ever seen in her life.

'Vivienne, come away from there!' Grace said, finally escaping her third lot of well-wishers. 'You're forever at it, peering in at those shoes, and the rest of the time you're prattling on about them at home! You should have more tact. It's not very nice for Mum to have to listen to you bleating about how everyone at school has shoes like that when you know very well she can't afford to buy you new ones.'

'I can't help it – they're so gorgeous! Oh Grace, don't you think they're gorgeous? They're called court shoes, like page-boys used to wear. Nancy Tuckett's got a pair and so's Marjorie Powell and Jeanette Everett and . . . oh, just about everyone in town!'

'They're not even practical – they're party kind of shoes. You just cut it out, Vivienne. It's going to be even tougher for Mum now I'll be away, because she relied on my board money. So just stop carrying on about those shoes, don't even think about them any more.'

It was difficult not to think about them. Getting off the bus at the hospital stop with a heavy load of groceries, Vivienne saw two more girls wearing those beautiful court shoes. She walked backwards, staring at the girls' feet, and a bag of sugar fell from the carton and burst.

'How could you be so clumsy, child!' Mum cried, looking aghast at the loss. 'You know we've got all those extra people coming tomorrow. Oh, what a wicked waste!'

'I tripped,' Vivienne said, feeling awful about the sugar scattered over the road. 'I came over a bit dizzy when I got off the bus . . .'

'You didn't,' Grace whispered. 'I saw you – you were craning around to look at those shoes the Sylvester girls had on. You'd just better remember what I said – not one more word to poor old Mum about them, or else!'

It was true, Vivienne thought guiltily. She had chattered on about those shoes to Mum – hinting, it couldn't be called anything else. And Mum had finally bitten her head off, demanding to know if she thought that money grew on trees and to be thankful that she had shoes to wear at all, even if they had been passed down from Grace to Heather to Cathy before she inherited them.

Money was even more scarce than usual this Christmas. Usually Mum treated them all to a big packet of crystallised fruit, but this year there was none, as Vivienne found out when she unpacked the groceries. There were no bottles of soft drink, either, and home-made lemonade would have to do instead, but even with those restrictions, Christmas was still Christmas. Cathy and Heather had got out the box of old decorations and were pinning up paper chains in the lounge room, squabbling as usual about where they were to go. One chain snapped in a vicious tug-of-war, so Mum set them to work mopping the front steps and let Vivienne take over the decorations.

While she was up on the table pinning a lantern to the frame of Dad's beloved picture of the Battle of Waterloo, she suddenly felt a searing pain in one ear. She stood, gasping, cupping a hand over the pain while it welled and then thankfully subsided. No one could get sick at Christmas, it just wouldn't be fair! But after tea, which was just cold meat and salad because Mum wanted to get things ready for the visitors tomorrow, the pain surged back, magnified.

'Oh!' Vivienne yelped, shoving her plate away. 'Oh, Mum, I feel putrid! My ear . . .'

'Don't say "putrid", it sounds so uncouth,' Grace said.

'Her forehead feels warmish,' Mum said anxiously. 'I hope you're not starting an ear abscess, Viv.'

'She'll have to have it syringed up at the hospital,' Cathy said. 'What they do is they get this huge plunger thing, then they fill it up with scalding hot oil and squirt . . .'

'I can find plenty of jobs for children who don't act sympathetic towards someone in pain,' Mum said. 'Jobs like scrubbing down the lavatory seat with Lysol, for instance, and cleaning out the pot-cupboard.' Cathy shut up. 'Vivienne, you'd better go and lie down, love. I'll get you a hot-water bottle and you can hold it against your poor ear.'

'It's hot enough without a hot-water bottle!' Vivienne wailed. 'I feel all sweaty and I don't want to have to stay in bed! There's putting the stockings up and . . . and making the table look nice and getting everything ready for tomorrow. Cathy and Heather and Grace – they'll all be having fun and I won't!'

'Bed,' Mum said firmly. 'I don't want you coming down with something serious and have to pay money to the doctor all through an ounce of prevention now. Don't cry, there's a good girl. You can pop into my bed for a while as a special treat.'

Isobel, arriving uninvited to stay overnight because her mother was going to a Christmas Eve party, waved briefly through the bedroom door.

'Is your dad . . .' she asked.

'No he's not!' Vivienne said crossly, kicking away the stifling blanket and trying to find a cool spot in the big brass bed. As well as the red-hot needle sensation in her ear, her nose had begun to run, and she'd had to use three of Dad's khaki handkerchiefs. 'He sent word down by the mail van yesterday that he's been held up but he'll make it home for Christmas dinner.'

'Well, I guess he's not likely to throw things at me while Christmas dinner's going on,' Isobel said. 'Geeze, poor you, having to stay in bed. I'm not coming any closer. You could be coming down with something like anthrax or chicken-pox, and I'm not having my summer holidays ruined before they even got started. Hey Viv, look what I got from Bailey's!'

Vivienne took one look and pulled the sheet over her face so she could have a good howl. Isobel had treacherously bought a pair of those lovely fleurs-de-lis court shoes. They twinkled on her feet like stars.

'Cry-baby. I never bawl when I get crook. I always dust cornflour over my face and lie there with my eyes shut making out I'm at death's door. You get more attention that way, when they think you're going to croak,' Isobel said, and went out into the kitchen to drive Mum crazy with suggestions for making exotic things like duckling stuffing with nasturtium leaves and anchovies.

But everyone was too occupied to pay any attention to Vivienne. She tossed about in the rumpled bed and listened wanly to the Christmas preparations in which she had no part. Cathy, Isobel and Heather sang carols while they decorated the lounge-room with big bunches of flowers they'd pinched from the hospital garden. Carols about holly and ivy and snow . . . Vivienne groaned and wished she lived in a country where it snowed, where she could dive into a snowdrift and gain some relief from the heat that scalded her skin. Maybe it would be better to go and sleep on the veranda, but out there she'd have to contend with all the mosquitoes and the noisy squeaking of the fruit bats in the peach tree.

She winced every time the oven door was opened and a tray was slid in and out, the sound echoing relentlessly inside her head. The whole house was filled with the spiced fragrance of things baking, but she felt too sick to enjoy it. As well as the sore ear, runny nose and pounding headache, her throat had started to hurt. It was so painful she could hardly bear it, but when she called weakly for a drink of water, no one heard. Mum was too busy in the kitchen and Grace, softened by Christmas goodwill, had allowed the others into her room while she sorted out her belongings for going away next month.

'Mum, look what Grace gave me!' she heard Cathy squeal, running down the hall. 'That beaut little felt beanie, she said it's not smart enough for the city and she doesn't want it any more – so I could have it!'

Vivienne groped for another khaki handkerchief. She listened jealously while Heather was given a pair of white cotton crochet gloves and a hair-slide, and Isobel a bra. Isobel hooked it on over her dress and came bouncing excitedly into the front room to look at herself in the full-length mirror, snapping on the overhead light and plunging a shaft of chain lightning into Vivienne's eyes.

'Hey . . . you look all white – did you take my tip about the cornflour?' she said, standing sideways in front of the mirror and poking out the bra cups with her fingertips to examine the effect. Mum came in and shooed her away, peering at Vivienne's clammy face.

'I think I'd better fetch a basin in case you need it,' she said. 'And a couple of Aspros. Never mind, it's late and everyone else is off to bed now. The stockings are all up and everything else done, so you'll be able to get some sleep without that lot galloping all over the house. I'll be glad to get to bed myself. You can sleep in here tonight, seeing Dad's not home yet, but nip down the back first, because I don't want any wet mattresses, thanks very much.'

Vivienne tottered down the backyard on wobbly legs that felt as though they were filled with sauce. She came back through the lounge-room and looked at the lumpy stockings hanging from the mantelpiece, an extra one for Isobel seeing she was staying overnight. On the hearth underneath Mum's stocking there was a shape she recognised – the plate she and Grace had bought together. Grace had wrapped it beautifully in red tissue paper with silver ribbon and written 'To Mum, happy Christmas from Viv and Grace' on the gift label. Vivienne was pleased to find that her own name had been put first, though the writing jumped about alarmingly in front of her eyes. Oh, she felt so sick!

She remembered the stockings of last Christmas. Maybe God was punishing her by making her feel so ill this year, because last Christmas Eve she'd done something wicked. A parcel had come by post from Aunty Elsie and she'd secretly unwrapped it and looked at the various gifts it contained before they were placed in the stockings. She and Cathy had both been sent bangles, but the one for Cathy had a buckle clasp and was far superior, while hers had been a boring, plain band. So she'd rewrapped both bangles, swapping over the name tags before anyone discovered she'd been snooping, and Cathy had found that ordinary bangle in her stocking on Christmas morning.

The table was already set for dinner tomorrow. Mum had made a wonderful centrepiece wreath from glossy green paper and red plasticine berries, and it looked just like real holly. Matching glasses saved all year from peanut butter and lemon spread were set around the good damask tablecloth. So many place settings – Isobel's mum was coming for Christmas dinner, and so were the Baroongal Flats Mellings, the Dions from up river, and Aunty Cessie, Uncle Trip and Lindsay from East Wilgawa. Everyone was coming – and she'd probably miss out on it all and be up at the hospital having a syringe full of boiling hot oil squirted in her ear!

She crept unsteadily into the kitchen to get a drink of water. Everything was in order for tomorrow. The meat-safe dangled solidly from its chain, heavy with a big round of corned beef and another of cold roast beef. Dad's terrible puddings sat in their white cloths waiting to be boiled all morning and served up to anyone foolish enough to want to try them. The ice-chest was crammed with setting jellies and a port-wine trifle decorated with swirls of rich mock cream. She drank some iced water queasily, then reeled back to the front room and climbed in next to Mum.

Mum was putting curlers in her hair for the company tomorrow. She finished the last one and covered them all with a pink hair-net, then turned off the light. Vivienne nestled beside her, blinking tearily at the moonlight spilling through the bay window. Even the moonlight looked harsh and hot! She couldn't remember ever having felt so miserable and was glad of Mum's large billowing bulk, even though it took up most of the bed. She burrowed her sweating face into Mum's cushiony arm.

'You'll feel better in a day or so,' Mum said. 'Just wait patiently for it to pass, that's all you can do. And stop sooking. Dad'll call you a squalling sissy. If you don't stop sooking, your eyes will look like burnt holes in a blanket when he comes home in the morning.'

'Maybe he won't even get back in time for Christmas . . .' Vivienne said wretchedly. 'He could have fallen down one of those old mine shafts while he's been off prospecting . . . There might have been a flood up there and he can't get Digger across the river. Or like in that poem where the drover's trying to get across the swirling torrent . . . and his dog tries to save him and drowns, and then right at the end there's just the pack horse left to bear sad tidings home! Oh, Mum!'

'A flood in summer, don't be so daft,' Mum said. 'And that ratbag Bluey wouldn't ever be any good at saving anyone, he's too scared of water. Dad's always got to hoist him up in front of him on the saddle when they're crossing streams. Your dad will get home all right. You wouldn't catch that one missing out on boiling up those awful puddings and making everyone tuck in, would you? Cheer up, you might find the lucky threepence in your slice.'

'A bushfire . . . A big tree fallen on him . . . Bitten by a snake and lying in the bush with no one knowing . . .'

'Hush now, Viv, don't go meeting trouble, there's plenty of it around without going looking for it. Just be patient and wait. He'll be home soon as he can get here, he's never missed a Christmas yet. Anyhow, there's no snake would dare bite your dad.'

'Sing us a song,' Vivienne whimpered through her pain, and Mum sang softly in the moonlight.

'"Come little leaves, said the wind one day.
Out in the meadow with me to play.
Put on your dresses of red and gold,
Summer has gone and the wind is cold . . ."'

'That's *sad*, that song,' Vivienne whispered.

'You never said so before. It's the song I always sang you kids to sleep with when you were babies, starting with Grace. It seems only yesterday I was rocking Gracie off to sleep, and now she's all grown up and . . . You always liked that song, Viv.'

'But now it's sad, because of Grace going away and the tung-oil nut plantation went broke and I won't have Cathy on the bus with me any more because she's going off to high school and I'm going to have boiling hot oil in my ear for Christmas and everything's . . . putrid!' Vivienne said and bawled desperately into the vast front of Mum's pink cotton nightie.